Queen of Disguises

Melanie Jackson

ORCA BOOK PUBLISHERS

Library and Archives Canada Cataloguing in Publication

Jackson, Melanie, 1956-
Queen of disguises / written by Melanie Jackson.

(A Dinah Galloway mystery)
ISBN 978-1-55469-037-4

I. Title. II. Series: Jackson, Melanie, 1956- . Dinah Galloway mystery.

PS8569.A265Q38 2009   jC813'.6   C2009-900014-8

First published in the United States, 2009
Library of Congress Control Number: 2008943722

Summary: Competing for a spot in a commercial, Dinah must become healthy
while eluding a vengeful pursuer.

Orca Book Publishers gratefully acknowledges the support for its publishing
programs provided by the following agencies: the Government of Canada
through the Book Publishing Industry Development Program and the Canada
Council for the Arts, and the Province of British Columbia through the BC Arts
Council and the Book Publishing Tax Credit.

Cover design by Lynn O'Rourke and John van der Woude
Mask photo credit by Dreamstime

Orca Book Publishers
PO Box 5626, Stn. B
Victoria, BC Canada
V8R 6S4

Orca Book Publishers
PO Box 468
Custer, WA USA
98240-0468

www.orcabook.com
Printed and bound in Canada.
Printed on 100% PCW recycled paper.
12 11 10 09 • 4 3 2 1

In memory of my mother, Pearl Chandler,
a true pilgrim soul.
MJ

A Vengeful Prelude

Game's on, Dinah Galloway.

Oh, not shot put or the hundred-meter dash or speed skating or any other sport you'd find at the Olympics. Mine's the revenge *game. A game of hide-and-seek, where I'm* It *and you're the target. The one I hunt down. And when the game's over, you won't sing or snoop anymore.*

That'll be a gold-medal day for me, Violet Bridey. That's right. VIOLET BRIDEY. The one you cruelly called Beak-Nose. Remember? Hmph! I happen to think a prominent bump is distinctive: gives one that Matterhorn look. Most imposing.

But back to the delicious revenge I'm plotting. All those months in prison, I nurtured my plan as tenderly as the begonia I kept on my windowsill. Pruned it back when it grew too much in the wrong direction; enriched it when it withered.

Not much else for me to do there except grow things. The begonia: an orange one, the color of fire. The idea: ink dark, cold as revenge.

Your fault I was an inmate, Dinah. You poked your freckled—and, if I may say so, rather snub—nose, with those ever-smudged glasses teetering crookedly on top, into my oh-so-lovely plans. I had my fortune, that glowing moonstone, in the palm of my hand. How cleverly I'd stolen it, you must admit.

Then a scream from you, and the police were alerted. The prison walls closed around me.

The other inmates thought the walls were brick, but I knew better. The walls hemming me in were you. Your face was on every one of them. You, "the red-hot redhead," as critics drooled.

As they never drooled for me. "Too melodramatic," they sniffed. "No matter how hard she tries, she'll always be an amateur. Couldn't act her way out of a Theater for Dummies book!"

Yet even the critics had to acknowledge my particular talent. They never knew when I took on more than one role in a play, not till the end, when the lights came up. How I savored their eyes, bulging with astonishment; their slack jaws. It was all I could do not to laugh out loud at them as I took my bow for my multiple roles.

You see, Dinah, I am the Queen of Disguises. And now I've figured out the ultimate *disguise, hee hee. That's how I'll avenge myself on you.*

Prepare to meet your own personal It, Dinah Galloway. Your curtain call.

Chapter One

A Stalker...But Where?

"LET THE GAMES BEGIN!"

A voice blasted out of the loudspeaker right over our heads. I jumped, bumping Madge.

"You're so jittery today, Dinah," my sister scolded. "Anyone would think you'd developed a nervous twitch. Especially in your neck. Why do you keep looking behind us?"

"I don't know. It's weird. I have this feeling someone's watching me." I craned round again, surveying the dozens of other kids waiting, like me, for an audition to sing in commercials for Vancouver's 2010 Olympics. Two of us would be chosen: one for a commercial featuring opera, one for swing.

Swing, a-ring-a-ding-ding, as Sinatra would say. That'd be me. I hoped.

The other kids, and the SAs (i.e., significant adults) accompanying them, were staring anxiously at the door of the Witherspoon Advertising Agency. When Mr.

Witherspoon deigned to open it, we'd be called, one by one, to go in and sing.

The loudspeaker re-erupted. "LET THE GAMES BEGIN!"

Some of the younger auditioners started crying. The volume was set so *loud*. According to a secretary who had popped out earlier, the repeated announcement was supposed to rev us up. Put us in mind of athletes slaloming down hills and so on. But it was merely deafening us. I and a lot of the other kids stuffed our fingers in our ears.

Madge didn't need to. She had her iPod on and was test-listening to different pieces of music for her wedding, planned for the end of August. Madge was the only person in the crammed hall with a blissed-out smile.

As usual, male glances fluttered and settled on her like hungry bees. My eighteen-year-old sister was a drop-dead stunner. She had creamy skin, softly wavy auburn hair and lupine-blue eyes with—get this—long, *naturally dark* eyelashes, as compared to my stubby reddish ones.

Maybe I had the feeling of being watched today because of Madge. Maybe I'd intercepted some of the stares meant for her.

An elbow like a wrecking ball knocked me aside. It belonged to a pale, slick-haired, practically lipless boy my size. That is to say, shorter than your average tween. Reaching up a tuxedoed arm, he plucked one of Madge's earphones off.

"Hey, baby," he greeted her, pitching his voice low. "Can you give me directions? I'm lost in love."

"Um," I said nervously. The kid looked like Countlet Dracula, but I felt I ought to warn him. "Madge isn't the most patient—"

"Quiet, Pee Wee," the kid said out of the corner of his mouth.

To my astonishment, Madge broke into a lovely smile. "You're so sweet," she cooed to the kid. "Interrupting my appreciation of Debussy."

He flapped his eyebrows at her. "In the next room, it'll soon be my *début, see*? Ha ha ha."

"So cute," Madge smiled.

And, grasping his shirt and tuxedo collar all at once, she hoisted the kid and jammed him in a nearby wastebasket. "Weight lifting pays off," she remarked to me. Then, calmly, she replaced the dangling earphone and listened on.

Madge was talented at tuning the world out, even when she wasn't iPod-equipped. My sister was a dreamy artist who floated through much of her life musing about how to portray beauty in urban settings. The grimier, the better. This was her specialty, what she described as putting opposite ideas together, the clash before the creation. Uh, oka-a-a-ay. Anyhow, I was secretly quite proud of Madge. She'd be starting next month at the Emily Carr University of Art and Design.

"Oh, Cornwall," gushed a big, platinum-dyed-haired woman in a black-and-white check dress. Shoving other auditioners and SAs out of the way, she lumbered over to him. "Your nice tux, son! You *promised* to be careful."

She tried unwedging Cornwall from the basket. Then—

"AUDITIONS WILL BEGIN SHORTLY. WE WILL CALL FOR SINGERS IN ALPHABETICAL ORDER."

Startled, Cornwall's mother fell backward, knocking over a fat, cherubic little boy and girl. Carl and Carlotta Featherwhist, the Singing Toddler Twins. I'd got to know

Carl, Carlotta and their mom at auditions; I even babysat the twins sometimes. They were good kids, if a little hyper.

Flattened by Cornwall's mother, the twins now erupted into wails.

Over the heads of some SAS, I spotted the telltale neon orange of a snack machine. Using my head as a battering ram, I plowed through the crowd. Madge had *her* music; I had mine. In this case, the sound of a package of Fudgee-Os crashing to the vending machine slot.

As I tucked two chocolaty cookies in my mouth at once, a finger timidly tapped my shoulder. I turned, face bulging, to see a thin girl with long, neatly combed chestnut hair. She peered at me shyly out of large, dark eyes.

"Angela Bridey!" I got out, more or less.

It was kind of an awkward moment, since I'd helped send her Aunt Violet to jail the previous fall for attempting to steal a valuable moonstone ring. But then, I thrive on awkward moments. They're so much more interesting than regular ones.

I gulped down the Fudgee-Os and smiled at Angela. After all, what's a little family incarceration between friends? "I know you'll impress Mr. Witherspoon with your beautiful high soprano," I said sincerely. "Though maybe he should remove any crystalware from the room before you start."

Angela crumpled into tears. "Oh, Dinah!"

"I was just kidding," I said in alarm. "Jokes are kind of a reflex with me." I glanced round. With one hand on his neck, another on his ankles, the platinum-haired woman was trying to wrench Cornwall from the wastebasket. The twins kept on howling.

"THE 2010 OLYMPICS: A TIME FOR BRITISH COLUMBIANS TO COME TOGETHER."

I hoped no members of the International Olympics Committee would be dropping by Witherspoon Advertising anytime soon. "Er, Angela…"

She grabbed my shoulder to steady herself. "Dinah, I have terrible news. Aunt Violet has escaped prison—*and she's coming after you!*"

I gulped. My throat dried up like a late-autumn leaf, not the greatest development for a singer about to audition. I plunked more change into the machine for a reviving can of coconut-flavored root beer.

"I'm into gourmet foods," I explained as Angela stared at the can. "But please, tell me more about Aunt Vi's real-life episode of *Prison Break*."

Angela shook her head sorrowfully. "All those months in prison, she ranted about you, Dinah. Said she would come for you. Like *It*."

"Oh, well, if it's a game of hide-and-seek she wants…" I shrugged. But I was rattled. I remembered Violet Bridey's small, ruthless black eyes darting greedily around for the priceless moonstone she came very close to stealing—until I exposed her in front of hundreds of people at the Livingston Theater in Vancouver. I remembered Violet's furious shrieks, and her beak nose quivering, like an arrow seeking a bull's eye, over the shoulders of the police who bore her away.

I also remembered uncomfortably that in long-ago games of hide-and-seek, little Dinah was always the first kid spied by *It*. My flaming red hair advertised my whereabouts.

Plus, I was then, as now, loud and energetic.

My mother, who's a librarian and irritatingly fond of quotations, says that, noisy as I am, I'll never suffer the "lives of quiet desperation" that others do, heading "to the grave with the song still in them." I should say not! I'm with my idol, the late Judy Garland, who told her Carnegie Hall audience she was willing to "sing 'em all and stay all night." *Yessss*.

Carnegie Hall, in New York. *Crumbly* Hall I called it when I was little. Singing there one day, like Judy, was my dream.

Sigh. My reality was that I sang radio commercials for Sol's Salami on West 4th. I'd performed on a TV show amid flying lemon meringue pies and recorded a movie title tune with a barking dog. Between such stellar gigs, I trundled off to endless crowded auditions like this one. Overnight success? Over-millennium it sometimes felt like.

For now I had to stem the flood of tears gushing down Angela's cheeks. I turned the hide-and-seek reminiscence into a joke to cheer Angela up.

She only cried harder. Geez. *Girls.* "It's okay," I consoled her. "I'm not afraid. Really. I'm sure the police will catch your Aunt Vi."

"BLUTZ, CORNWALL," the loudspeaker blasted.

The door to Witherspoon Advertising opened. Cornwall was only half out of the wastebasket, so his mother ended up rolling him in.

Angela reached into the pocket of her black velvet dress for a white, ironed handkerchief folded into a neat square. "The police might *not* catch Aunt Vi, Dinah. She's the Queen of Disguises." Angela dabbed at her eyes with a corner of the hanky. I knew—I just *knew*—she was reluctant to wrinkle it. She was that type of girl.

Angela wept, "Just when the disgrace to our family was dying down, Dinah! Now we'll be in the headlines again. It's so embarrassing. For ages after Aunt Vi's trial, I couldn't go to auditions: the Bridey name was too notorious. Mommy, who's always pushing me to succeed, was *ballistic*.

"Good thing Mommy can't see me—she'd fret that I was spoiling my appearance by crying. She went off to shop at the Bay rather than wait." Angela mopped her eyes some more. "Anyhow, the kids at school were so *mean* during Aunt Vi's trial. They said that, with a criminal in the family, I couldn't possibly be called *Angela*. They started calling me *Devilla*."

"That's just cheap, immature humor," I responded. Though, having a weakness for cheap, immature humor myself, I had to bite the inside of my lower lip not to laugh. Devilla!

It would've been nervous laughter, I grant you.

"BRIDEY, ANGELA."

Everyone in the hall jumped. Someone in a carrot outfit smashed against me, treading heavily on my foot. "Wanna get shredded?" I asked crossly.

Then I grabbed Angela's hanky and wiped down her face with it. "You're on," I told her. "Dazzle them with your mighty soprano, and forget Beak—" I realized that Angela had the same pronounced nose as her aunt. "Er, forget about Aunt Vi. She's irritating, but not important." I shoved Angela through the door.

Same goes for you, I coached myself as beautiful high notes began cascading through the door into the hall. Don't worry about Beak-Nose Bridey. Think of her as a tiny, insignificant pest. Gnat-like.

I was making good psychological progress with this when Madge rushed up to me. "Dinah!" my sister cried, enveloping me in a protective hug that accidentally jammed a headset earpiece into my left nostril. "I've had a call from Mother—*you're in great danger!*"

Mother had just heard from the police about Violet Bridey's escape.

As Beak-Nose was middle-aged and the moonstone theft was a first offense, the judge had sentenced her to a minimum-security prison. One you could, in a half-decent disguise, slip out of. All these months, while the milkman delivered eggs, Vi was hatching plans. She'd quietly cut and sewn sheets into a white uniform; yesterday she'd dashed out to the milk truck, jump-started the ignition and roared off.

Madge reported breathlessly, "Before she escaped, Beak-Nose bragged about how she was going to avenge herself, how she was coming after you. She—"

I held up a hand wearily. "I know, I know. I heard about it from Angela. Beak-Nose was not spouting Hallmark wishes for my health and well-being."

Madge bent to examine my face. "You're kind of white under your freckles, Dinah. I didn't mean to scare you. Well, maybe I did, a bit," she admitted, "so that you'll be careful till Beak-Nose is caught!" Another squishy sisterly hug.

"FEATHERWHIST, CARL AND CARLOTTA!"

It was the twins' turn. Their mother herded them in, urging them not to sniffle on their matching sailor outfits.

Madge herself was looking somewhat teary, so I rummaged in my jacket pocket for my version of Angela's starched hanky, a used Kleenex, to give her.

Instead my fingers closed on a folded piece of paper. Huh? My jacket, the dark green one I wear to all auditions because Mother and Madge think it flatteringly sets off my red hair, had only come back from the dry cleaner's the day before. There hadn't been time for me to accumulate my usual candy wrappers and reminders to myself that I never remembered to read.

I pulled the paper out and unfolded it. Letters were scrawled in wiggly capitals:

YOU'RE FRESH OUT OF ENCORES, DINAH GALLOWAY. TAKE YOUR FINAL BOW.

—YOUR PERSONAL IT, VIOLET BRIDEY.

Chapter Two

Stage Fright

"That carrot," I burbled. "That person who bashed into me a minute ago. *It was Violet Bridey*. She stuffed the note in my pocket."

I began bouncing on my toes, straining my five-foot frame to see if the carrot-outfitted person was still in the room. Why, oh why did I have to be puny? By mistake I kicked someone in the heel. "Sorry, I'm looking for a carrot."

"Try a greengrocer's," the man snapped. Inclining protectively over a girl in a fluffy pink tutu, he urged, "Ignore that loud girl, Wilhemina. She's known for attracting attention to herself. Why, the moment that salami commercial comes on, I have to rush to the radio to switch the volume down. Most unseemly," he sniffed.

Madge peered round the hall. Being tall, this was easier for her. "Beak-Nose must've slipped out. No carrot in sight," she reported.

The man shot Madge an angry scowl and turned

back to his daughter. "*Concentrate*, Wilhemina. Be in the dramatic moment."

"You're not safe here, Dinah," Madge said, clutching my hand as if I were a helium balloon apt to fly loose at any moment. "No audition is that important. We're leaving."

I gulped. "I can't walk out of an audition, Madge. Mr. Wellman's sure I'll get the swing-singing job. He's so excited."

Mr. Wellman's my agent. He puts up with a lot from me, as I tend to get entangled in mysteries. Mr. Wellman carries a container of Tylenol around at all times, except that he calls it *Di*-lenol, for all the headaches I give him. But he says that when I sing, it's worth it all. The sound for the fury.

Even in my nervousness about Beak-Nose, Queen of Disguises, I could still imagine the thrill of representing British Columbia and the 2010 Olympics in commercials broadcast across Canada, the United States and even Europe! I had to audition. I owed it to Mr. Wellman, to Madge, who'd come with me, to this weird ability I have to fill every possible corner with my voice. Though what I'm really sending out is my heart.

And if I got the job, there'd be no more singing while dogs barked or pies flew. I'd be big-time! An Olympics-commercial gig could lead to Carnegie Hall.

"GALLOWAY, DINAH."

Mr. Witherspoon, showing off his tanned muscles in a blue satin tank top and gym shorts, was jogging round a huge mahogany desk. I wasn't sure whether to greet him or tell him to heel. His secretary was clocking him with a stopwatch.

"Two minutes, Edgar," she intoned. "Two point three five."

The advertising agency president rounded the desk yet again. "Sorry," he called vaguely in our direction. "When you represent the Olympics, you *have* to be in shape."

Then he noticed Madge and collided with a corner of the desk. "*Owwww*." He winced as a diagonal red welt appeared on one thigh. He didn't stop gaping at her, though. "You're Dinah Galloway? I've heard you sing about salamis—I thought you were younger, somehow. It's only kids we're supposed to be auditioning, but"— Mr. Witherspoon hopped on his unwounded leg over to Madge—"I'm free for dinner tonight, and we could—"

"No, we couldn't," Madge said icily. "And *this* is Dinah Galloway. I'm Dinah's accompanist today."

She slid onto the piano bench. Flushing, Mr. Witherspoon hopped to his desk chair and collapsed.

Madge tinkled out the intro to "Get Happy," the swing tune I'd be performing. A hit for Judy Garland, its fast-paced, optimistic mood seemed perfect, since this was an audition to show how cheery and rah-rah you could be. *Make people realize what a fun bunch we British Columbians are*, Mr. Wellman had coached me. *Make them want to come visit us.*

But I wasn't feeling as I had during practice sessions, bouncy and happy like the song. I was feeling terrified. An escaped convict was hunting me down. Her beak nose had already scented me out, and she'd slipped a threatening note into my pocket. While in the guise of a clumsy carrot.

The shaking in my teeth spread all over me. What was next, a vengeful rutabaga?

"I c-can't," I chattered.

Madge stopped mid-note. Nursing his thigh, Mr. Witherspoon stared at me, his mouth edging into an impatient line. His thin assistant scowled.

I tried to find a fresh area of lower lip that I hadn't chewed. I looked away, anywhere but at the disapproving ad agency duo.

Against one wall, on a row of chairs that ended at a long curtain, sat several people holding clipboards. I remembered Mr. Wellman telling me that there'd be some BC government officials at the auditions, an Olympics promotional committee that would decide on the finalists. These people didn't look fierce. One woman, plump and rosy, winked encouragingly at me. "Don't be scared," she mouthed.

But I *am* scared, I thought. How can I sing "Get Happy"? My singing instructor always tells me to put my feelings into my voice so I'm not just volume, *volume*, VOLUME. Otherwise I won't be believable in what I'm singing.

Unsure what to do, Madge twirled her engagement ring on her finger. Mr. Witherspoon rose, balancing his weight on his uninjured leg. "Look, we're tight for time. If you can't—"

"I can't," I agreed and gulped. I couldn't be believable singing a happy song, not the way I was feeling now.

"I'll call the next auditioner," the secretary said. With a piercing scratch, she penned a line through my name on the clipboard she was carrying.

I thought, But I can be believable singing a scared song.

"Change of song selection," I blurted at Madge. "We'll do—we'll do 'The Night Has a Thousand Eyes.'"

"Um...I don't actually know how to play that, Dinah."

"I do!" The plump, rosy woman leaped up and wriggled her hips. "Hooo-eee! We jived to 'Thousand Eyes' at high school. One of my favorites!" She plunked down on the piano bench; Madge just had time to scramble away before being knocked off.

The woman crashed into the opening notes right away. Not quite my key, so my first words out were kind of flat. But a song about someone being watched by someone else *could* start out nervous. The woman adjusted the key downward for me and I plowed on.

Then I started getting into the beat of the music. I always do. The beat lifts me up, dances me away, like the Pied Piper. Chasing the beat, I'm all voice, all heart, pure joy—even singing a sad, or in this case strange and paranoid, song.

> *So remember when you tell those little white lies*
> *That the night has a thousand eyes!*

I sang in jumpy notes, accelerating the song's already quick beat. The committee grew jumpy too. Their feet started tapping, their hands slapped their sides, their heads bobbed. Even cool, unflappable Madge, who'd taken the seat the woman vacated, was bouncing on the spot.

"*Remember when you tell those little white lies…*"

One by one the other committee members slid off their chairs, got up and danced. Madge beamed.

"Well!" The woman at the piano crashed the lid down with finality. "I think we have our swing singer!"

Her colleagues, hot from dancing, paused in removing their jackets and mopping their foreheads with them to applaud.

"But, Mrs. Beechum," Mr. Witherspoon objected, in a tone pitched high with annoyance, "what about my nephew? You clapped for him too."

"Now, Edgar," Mrs. Beechum said, after pausing to give me a high five, "we have the next red-hot mama of show business here. Your nephew can be runner-up, second in line to Dinah. Her understudy."

Screech! The curtain beside the farthest chair was wrenched aside. Cornwall Blutz stomped in, his slicked hair catching the overhead light and flashing it angrily about the room.

I remembered something else Mr. Wellman had told me about the audition. The semifinalists, those the committee was impressed with, would be bundled into a side room for further consideration. With only a curtain to separate us, Cornwall had heard every word. He glowered at me.

Never mind a thousand eyes. These were two deadly ones.

"Don't worry," Mrs. Beechum murmured, escorting Madge and me to the elevator. She pushed out her hands, forcing the other auditioners and their SAs apart, like Moses and the Red Sea. "I'm the committee chairwoman. Edgar knows quite well I can whisk the Olympics promotional campaign away from him. He'll grumble, but you'll get the job. Don't give Edgar or his nephew a second thought."

But I gave them fourth, fifth and sixth thoughts, at least, as Madge and I waited on the platform of the Granville SkyTrain station. Not to mention thinking about the ominous Beak-Nose, with her cunning vegetable disguises. "I'm supposed to sing about how friendly British Columbia is, but it doesn't *feel* friendly," I told Madge.

"Think about my wedding," she counseled. "That'll be friendly." And she heaved a deep romantic sigh.

Madge and her fiancé, Jack French, would have a small wedding, a few friends and family. Oh, the plans had started out big, with the date set far in the future and gazillions of relatives, caterers and florists involved. The plans had ballooned to 2010 Olympics proportions, you might say—and at that point Madge and Jack nixed them. Jack's sister, Mrs. Rinaldi, who'd been organizing the grand plans, was still in a huff.

"Okay," I said, with such sudden agreeableness that Madge narrowed her lupine blues in suspicion. But I was thinking that wedding talk would distract my sister from fears about Beak-Nose. I really didn't want to be enveloped in any more tearful hugs today.

"You'll be a knockout bridesmaid in the dark green dress with the tulle neck and sleeves that I'm making for you," Madge glowed.

My sister does have elegant taste, I'll give her that. Because she and Jack, being students, didn't have much money, she was designing and sewing her own wedding dress too. Madge wouldn't let anyone else see the dress, not even Mother. She worked on it in the attic and locked the door behind her, like a mad scientist.

I told Madge this, and she laughed. Madge had mellowed over the past months. Goddess-like in looks and behavior, she used to be uptight about flaws in other people. Then, thanks to yours truly, she met Jack, who was easygoing and teased her out of her perfectionism.

Plus, she'd co-experienced, or maybe she'd view it as co-*endured*, some of my recent adventures. Madge was more understanding about those of us who weren't quite at the goddess level, like her. More relaxed. For example, she didn't flinch anymore at the mention of Dad, who'd died seven years ago, drunk, when he'd slammed his car into a tree.

Far down in the tunnel, there was a rumble. The train was coming. We and the rest of the crowd on the platform moved forward from the gleaming gray walls, closer to the tracks. The first rush of wind burst into the station, tickling my skin and ruffling my hair, which I'd combed into a dark red sheen. Madge wasn't the only one who was changing. I actually took some care of my appearance these days. Not a lot, but I didn't look quite so harum-scarum as I used to.

Dazzling silver lights filled the tunnel. The train hurtled toward us, the wind gathering itself into a blast—

And I felt a hand at my back, shoving me onto the tracks.

Chapter Three

Pantelli's Not-So-Dazzling Feat

"But you saw no one," said Constable Fanshawe, jotting on her pad.

"No. Or rather," I gulped, wishing the scene weren't quite so blurred in my mind, the train rushing at me in a gust of silvery wind, Madge heaving me back by the collar, "I saw *lots* of people, all around me."

Too many to separate any particular one from the others, the one who'd shoved me. With a chorus of screams, people had pressed around Madge and me, gaping, their faces stretched into grotesque extremes of shock, worry, fear…

"The transit police questioned people," said Constable Fanshawe, an unsmiling, though not unkind, young woman with a cloud of dark curly hair. "No one noticed a beak-nosed woman." The constable raised her eyebrows at me; I'd briefed her on the human carrot. "In any shape or form," she added dryly.

Then Jack, huddled protectively beside me on one end of our faded chintz sofa, with Madge on the other, objected. "The transit cops didn't question everyone. They have no authority to detain people. Violet Bridey could've walked calmly out of the station." In frustration he ran a hand through his sandy hair. "Heck, given the singular lack of observant witnesses, she could've *flown* out without attracting attention."

"It's a bird, it's a plane, it's Super Beak," I muttered.

"SUPER BEAK!" yelled my co-best friend Pantelli Audia. He found the name catchy and had been blasting it from his lungs for the past half hour or so. "SUPER BEAK!" He swung from branch to branch on the huge horse-chestnut tree outside our house.

Pantelli was deeply into trees. Sometimes I pretended to check his skin to see if bark was forming. He wanted to be a dendrologist—that is a tree specialist—when he grew up.

"SUPER BEAK!"

Not that the votes had come in yet on whether Pantelli actually *would* grow up.

Madge appeared on the upstairs balcony. "Pantelli, I'm waiting for the florist to bring me a sample corsage for my going-away dress—and I'd prefer that she not be frightened off." Madge floated back into her bedroom. Vaguely we heard her blathering that the florist was convinced a deep violet would be the best color.

My soon-to-be brother-in-law was setting up the sprinkler to douse the young cedars he'd planted across the front edge of our yard. Jack paused to shoot an amused and adoring look up at the balcony. A going-away dress, Madge had explained to us, was what the bride wears when she and the groom head off on their honeymoon.

Theirs would be a short honeymoon, just over the Labor Day weekend. They had to come back to school right after, Madge to Emily Carr, Jack to the University of British Columbia. Their actual honeymoon destination was as yet undecided: they were still trying to figure out what they could afford.

"Deep violet, huh?" murmured Jack, shaking his head.

My other co-best friend, Talbot St. John, and I were singing "Froggy Went A-Courtin." Talbot was strumming his guitar. We were both pitching our voices low and gravelly to sound like Bruce Springsteen when he sings "Froggy" on his album *We Shall Overcome*.

"HE WENT DOWN TO MISS MOUSEY'S DEN, UH-HUH, UH-HUH..."

Talbot was an ace guitarist. He could play any type of music—folk, rock, old standards (what I usually sing, the ones my dad taught me) or classical. He could play 'em sweeter than sweet or hotter than wicked, depending on his mood. Talbot wanted to be a poet-songwriter-musician when *he* grew up—though, due to his solemn conscientiousness, I sometimes thought he'd been grown-up since birth.

Pantelli stopped swinging. All we could see of him were his legs, dangling rather thoughtfully through the thick green leaves and spiky, brilliant green chestnut husks. "Yo, Jack," he called. "You want to aim the water just shy of those babies. That way, they'll stretch their roots and grow faster."

Jack straightened. It was a hot day, and he'd already weeded the flowerbeds and mowed the front and back lawn. His T-shirt was soaked with sweat.

Pantelli's helpful tree tip was about the tenth he'd tossed down. Jack frowned at the scuffed running shoes swaying at his eye level. He started to say something. Talbot and I muted our singing to listen; it's always fun when adults break into exactly the type of language they forbid you to use.

Jack caught himself. "Thanks, buddy," he said shortly.

"That corrective tree info is just the type of wisdom I intend to share at school," Pantelli said chattily. "I'm going to start a young dendrologists' club. I've already e-mailed the principal. Can't wait till the start of school. Only one month away."

"And *I* intend to start a history club if there isn't one," Talbot was saying. "I'd like to organize a special project, maybe a public display, on the history of the Olympics. Do you guys know how the Olympics originated?"

"No," Pantelli and I both responded unenthusiastically.

That was Talbot's other interest: history, of any time, any place. Oh, not that I minded his lectures. A lot of what Talbot told me was fascinating. Especially the gruesome stuff, like kings and queens getting beheaded. Did you know that Mary, Queen of Scots' lips kept moving, even after her severed head rolled off the chopping block? Maybe she was tossing out a wisecrack about her captors— you gotta assume it was a one-liner.

But sometimes, as now, I wanted to bypass the history lessons and sing. I decided to let Talbot know this via a subtle hint.

"WITHOUT MY UNCLE RAT'S CONSENT," I belted out.

Talbot was undeterred. "Oxylos, an ancient Greek king, is said to have come up with the idea of the Olympic Games. His descendant, Ifitos, really got the discus rolling, you might say. He figured his kingdom, Elis, and its neighbors, Sparta and Pisa, needed a break from constant wars. So Ifitos drew up a treaty with those countries, a sacred truce, in 776 BC. As long as the games were on, ix-nay on any fighting. People would strive to be the best they could be, as opposed to the worst, which wars brought out."

Jack had been shoveling mulch over the base of our new trees. He paused to lean on the shovel handle. "People striving to be the best they can be," he repeated, his gray eyes thoughtful. "That, or something like it, wouldn't be a bad campaign slogan."

Jack would be running as a Green Party candidate for city council in Vancouver's November elections. The youngest candidate ever. But he'd had lots of leadership experience—and just as important, he said, experience in getting people to compromise—what with heading up a save-the-spotted-owl group this summer, and an anti-smoking one last summer.

"Um, guys," I interrupted as Jack and Talbot blathered on about Olympic ideals, "I was hoping to practice some more singing before my old-age pension kicks in."

Talbot turned his solemn dark eyes on me. "But the stuff we're talking about, the spirit of the Olympics and all that, is what you'll be singing about, Dinah."

I clutched my hair till it stood up in wings. "Spirit, schmirit. Talbot, you know I can't stand it when you get theoretical."

A flash of yellow appeared between the young cedars: a cab was pulling up. We heard a door open. "Thank you, Mrs. Bridey," said a familiar oily voice.

"MRS. BRIDEY?" Pantelli yelped from the foliage. He swung himself way back; then, letting go of his branch, he launched forward in a fast, feet-first diagonal. With a bellow of "Yo, Super Beak!" he sailed over the cedars.

We heard a *thwack*, followed by a scream and a scuffle.

Jack plunged through the cedars he'd been nesting so carefully in the soil. Thrust aside, they bent into ten and two o'clock positions, respectively. Talbot and I peered through the gap.

Jack was helping a dark-haired but, more to the point, unbeak-nosed woman up from the sidewalk. Though the woman's skirt and jacket were mussed, the real damage was a shiny purple half-moon around her left eye. On top of the purple, you could just make out the imprint of Pantelli's heel.

"I'm afraid you're going to have quite a shiner," Jack said apologetically.

Pantelli scrambled up, dazed. "I should've had a better look at your nose before I launched myself," he told the shaken woman, whose eye was swelling up to baseball size.

However, Pantelli barely noticed. His gaze was glued to the other person who'd climbed out of the cab: Angela Bridey. A silly smile floated across Pantelli's face. "Hi," he breathed.

Uh-oh. The woman he'd struck was Angela's mother. The *other* Mrs. Bridey.

Madge called from the balcony, "Is that the florist with my deep violet corsage?"

"We're going to need an ice pack, darlin'," Jack yelled back.

"I *know* about keeping orchids frozen, Jack."

Just then the cab disgorged two more people: the owner of the oily voice, Cornwall Blutz, along with his mother.

"Dreadful way to greet someone," Mrs. Blutz huffed. Shoving Cornwall aside, she lumbered up to the other

Mrs. Bridey and gave her a bone-crunching hug. "Poor Dot. That purple hue doesn't suit you at all, dear."

Dot Bridey was bent double with the combined pain of shiner and hug. Slowly, gently, Jack led the hunched woman up the path toward our front door.

Angela sidled around Pantelli, who was ogling her with the sort of adoration he usually reserved for rare tree specimens like the Chinese Wingnut.

"I wanted to congratulate you, Dinah, on being the finalist for the swing-music commercial." She blushed. "I got the opera-commercial job. I was pretty sure I would, only because there weren't many other contenders. Most kids wanted to sing swing.

"Anyhow, it looks like we'll be spending a lot of time together over the next month, and I'm so glad. I've always wished I could be like you: so energetic, never a dull moment," Angela concluded.

"Time together…the next month?" I matched Angela's shy smile with an insincere one. I like girls, but in small doses. So often they end up being weird, cooing over hip-hugging jeans or plastic neon bracelets, or giggling too much, or uttering dainty *ewww*'s.

The cab's other passenger door swung open with a grating squeak. Mrs. Beechum got out, stuffing bills into the cab driver's hand. At the sight of me, she wiggled her hips and shouted, "Let's jive!"

She bounced toward me, beaming. "So exciting! A fitness retreat, Dinah. You and Angela, and Cornwall as your understudy."

I gaped. "I don't need an understudy."

Mrs. Beechum's head bobbed. "Didn't your agent get in touch with you? Oh, how awkward. He must not've got my message. Yes, Cornwall will be understudying you. Edgar Witherspoon insisted, in case you, er"—she mopped at her forehead with a tissue—"don't make it."

"Huh?" I felt my veins doing a fast chill. By *don't make it*, did she mean, in case Beak-Nose got me first?

Mrs. Beechum hesitated. Angela dropped her eyelids. Cornwall and his mother smirked at each other.

Talbot reached the same lurid conclusion I had. He stomped through the cedars and brandished his guitar as if it were a baseball bat. "If that Beak-Nose dame comes anywhere near Dinah, I'll—"

"What? No, nothing to do with that dreadful escaped convict," Mrs. Beechum protested, horrified. I was rather pleased by this angry display of Talbot's, but my good humor was squashed by the promotional committee chairwoman's next words.

"For the next month, you'll all three be going to a fitness retreat on Salt Spring Island. It's a condition of performing in the commercials: by shaping up, you'll set an example to other young British Columbians. And you, Dinah…" She sighed. "You'll have to trim down." In a confiding whisper she added, "Edgar doesn't think you'll be able to do it. He's sure Cornwall will get the job by default. But *I* have confidence in you."

I didn't. Lose weight? *Me?*

"B-but," I stammered, "I can't. I won't. Ho Hos depends on me."

Mrs. Beechum twisted her paper napkin in distress. "It'll be fine, Dinah. At the end of August, we committee members will visit the three of you on Salt Spring. We'll have a weigh-in to see if you've dropped, say, ten pounds, and—" She hesitated, then plunged on to get the unpleasantness over with fast, as if she were administering a needle. "We'll have a second, public tryout between you and Cornwall, to make it official. Oh, you'll win, Dinah. It's just to satisfy Edgar once and for all."

I was prepared to spew out more protests. However, at that moment, Madge came to the front door and found Jack and a hunched-over-in-pain Dot Bridey on the step.

"I bet you're the florist with my deep violet corsage," Madge said happily.

Dot Bridey raised her head, and her mottled, purple, baseball-sized shiner came into view.

Madge broke into a blood-curdling scream...

Chapter Four

Sinister Surprise at Trout Lake

"And you're marrying *into* this family?"

Mrs. Blutz's loud whisper to Jack swept the living room, where Mother and Mrs. Beechum were fussing over Dot Bridey with ice packs, aspirin and that Galloway cure for all ills, cups of tea. Even Wilfred the cat was helping. Wilfred, whose big fascination in life was dripping water, had planted himself at the injured woman's feet. As drops fell off the ice pack, he swiped at them with a fluffy white and pumpkin-pie-colored paw.

Pantelli had seated himself beside Angela and was presenting her with leaf samples from the plastic baggie he carried everywhere. "And this is a sample of the *Fraxinus excelsior*," he said, pressing a dried black bud into her palm. He glowed fondly at Angela. "You, a layperson, would know the tree as an ash."

"You're a bit of an ash yourself," sniped Cornwall from our ancient red velvet chair. He'd found the spring sticking out the side and was pulling on it. As a result, a rip was cascading down the entire side.

"Anytime you want to go outside, buddy," Talbot invited. Raising his guitar close to Cornwall's ear, he strummed deafeningly.

"I don't want to be any trouble," Angela's mom was bleating. "Really, I just want to go home."

"And I'll give you a lift," Mrs. Beechum said warmly. "Just as soon as Mrs. Galloway signs the release for Dinah to go to this diet-and-fitness retreat on Salt Spring."

"A fat farm," I said.

"What? Oh, no-o-o, dear," Mrs. Beechum twittered, plunking the ice pack by mistake on Dot Bridey's chin. "It's a fun place. So healthy. You'll love it. Sun, swimming—"

"Cottage cheese," I filled in, "and—don't tell me— wheat germ."

"And weigh scales," Madge added, with a cold, bright smile I'd never seen before. "Don't forget *that*, Mrs. Beechum. Along with the expectation that, every day, that scale needle must creep down a bit more toward zero."

"Oh, dear," the promotional committee chairwoman exclaimed, reddening, and she clapped the ice pack on her own forehead.

Quashing an ever-broadening smile, Jack cleared his throat. "I'm very pleased to be marrying into the Galloway family," he corrected Mrs. Blutz. "From my point of view, 'normal' is so...confining."

"I collected the bud last spring," Pantelli continued to Angela. "Possibly you're familiar with the mountain ash over on West 3rd, near the museum."

Cornwall snorted. "Welcome to Weirdsville."

I grabbed the dried bud from Angela, who was staring from it to Pantelli as if she'd stumbled onto the set of

Twilight Zone. Placing the bud on my fist, I flicked it with thumb and forefinger straight at Cornwall.

"Yeow!" he yelled, prying the bud out from between his eyelids.

Mrs. Blutz hurled herself at him with an anxious wail. To my surprise, no one reprimanded me. Mother was too busy tending to Dot Bridey's shiner, Mrs. Beechum was trembling before Madge's stare, and Jack rushed from the room with a sudden coughing fit.

Madge announced, "I, for one, object to the body-image police."

Soothing words, insults and strumming halted. This from calm, aloof Madge?

"Yes," said Madge, with a thin, amused smile. "Yes, Mrs. Beechum. I dispute your committee's right to dictate body image to my sister, or to anyone. I used to be a model. I happen to have, myself, the type of body advertisers like. I don't work at it; I was just born that way. A good part of the reason I gave modeling up was that I couldn't stand watching other girls whittle themselves down into a shape that advertisers dictated. We're all born looking our own way, not somebody else's, and we should celebrate these different ways."

Mrs. Beechum, boiling scarlet, tried to interrupt. Madge spoke louder. "Think about art," she said. "Would I, would anyone, find art so interesting if the only shape that existed was a long, thin, plank-like rectangle?"

Madge rose. She shot me a rather teary glance and then glared back at the government official. "Rejoice in my sister's *singing*, Mrs. Beechum. If you can't, you don't deserve her. In the long run it doesn't matter anyway. Dinah's goal is to sing at Carnegie Hall, and she'll get there, with or without this Olympics-commercial gig."

Madge then exited—into the wide-open arms that Jack had waiting for her in the hall.

"I've never been to a house where teatime is the equivalent of Hurricane Katrina!" groused Mrs. Blutz, stuffing Cornwall into the cab ahead of her.

Angela gave me one last, wistful glance. "I really hoped I'd get to spend a month on Salt Spring Island with you, Dinah. Now all I'll have for company is..."

She peeked into the cab, where Cornwall's slicked-back hair glistened, rather smugly, it seemed to me, in the sunlight pouring through the rear window. Angela was too tactful to finish her sentence.

Not me. "Cornbread?" I filled in loudly, and got a snarl from Cornwall in return. My adversaries and I like to maintain a high standard of witty exchanges.

Angela helped her moaning mother into the cab. Pantelli blocked them from view before I could say good-bye. "So," Pantelli said into the cab, "interested in visiting Van Dusen Gardens with me sometime, Ange? Van Dusen has—here, lemme give you a drumroll," he said as he pounded on the taxi's roof, "...*the largest selection of holly trees in Canada.*"

Pantelli zoomed off to create a wreath of twenty different types of bark for Angela. Madge gathered up my bridesmaid's dress, murmured something about adjustments and headed upstairs to the attic. Jack returned to gardening, and Mother went to phone my agent, Mr. Wellman, about turning down the Olympics commercials, with their fat-farm stipulation.

So life was normal again.

Except that, for some reason, I wasn't feeling talkative.

"Hey," said Talbot, stashing his guitar inside our front door, "let's go to Trout Lake."

At the south end of the lake, by the public beach, we bought Cokes and hot dogs from the concession stand. Grabbing packets of toppings, we wandered along the path to find a bench. We had to walk a long way because the beach area was crammed. Kids were hurling themselves into the lake, while their moms or older siblings watched and yelled at them to *be careful*.

Yup, just a normal Saturday in the 'hood.

Except…

"You sure are quiet, Di," said Talbot. We gave up trying to find a bench and sat on the overgrown dock about halfway along the east side of the lake, where it's marshy. "Are you sure you're okay?"

"Yeah." I shrugged. I ripped open toppings and began slathering them on my hot dog. Toppings *made* a dog in my view. I squished more and more mustard on till the hot dog resembled a yellow submarine. Huh. There was a song in that somewhere. I'd make millions.

I raised the hot dog to my mouth—and remembered Madge hurrying up the stairs with my green bridesmaid's dress. She'd pinned it together, slipped it over my head and then slipped it off again. The "adjustments" she'd murmured about making were of the expand, not contract, variety.

Talbot, better than anyone, knew my moods. Maybe that was why he was my best accompanist. He knew ahead of time how I was going to interpret a note, a line. Now he just looked at me understandingly from under the dark forelock that fell over his forehead. "When you do want to talk, ever, about anything, just let me know."

He popped the ring off the top of his Coke can. "Here," he said, handing the ring to me. "Elizabeth the First gave the Earl of Essex a ring for whenever *he* wanted to talk. All he had to do, the queen said, was send it to her, and she'd be there for him."

I held the oblong ring up and peered through it back at him as if it were a monocle. "Was that ring made of pop-can metal?" I kidded, though secretly I was pleased.

"Naw. The ring was made of some valuable jewel or other. But"—and Talbot gave one of my red hair strands a gentle tug—"when the earl eventually got into mega-trouble, he sent the valuable ring and the queen ignored it. *I* would show up if you needed me, and just for pop-can metal. So there."

Sounds of splashing reached us through the bulrushes. "We oughtta go swimming," Talbot suggested, chomping into his hot dog.

"Yeah." I studied my own mustard-saturated dog and felt my appetite ebbing away. Over the summer I'd made all kinds of excuses for not wanting to go swimming—fears of *E. coli*, possible Trout Lake monster sightings—and never admitted to myself the real reason. In a bathing suit, I'd resemble GM Place.

"Mr. Witherspoon was right about me: I'm fat," I blurted. "I'm a one-hundred-percent *bona fide* chubbette. You're the only person I'd tell that to, Talbot, and you're the person I least want to be fat with."

Unable to face him, I followed the path of some minnows doing figure eights around the lake weed. When I did peek up, he wasn't at all scornful. In fact, it seemed *his* turn to be pleased. Slowly I managed a wobbly grin to meet his warm one.

"Dinah," Talbot said, "forget Witherspoon. You always look great to *me* anyway."

I nodded, unable to speak. He stretched out his tanned, long, guitarist's fingers and laced them between my stubby, nail-bitten ones. And then the day became normal again, and I realized that normal was pretty wonderful.

Now that I felt better, my appetite returned like a trusty, if demanding, friend. I compromised between it and my reluctance to continue doubling for our local stadium by giving Talbot half my hot dog.

Except he never got to finish it. A huge, sopping, silver-furred dog leaped out of the marsh onto the dock and grabbed the final hot-dog wedge from Talbot's hand.

"Hi, London," we greeted her. London was our neighbors' silver husky. The Butterwicks had enrolled London in five different obedience-training programs without effect. She just had too much energy. She climbed trees and fences, invaded people's kitchens and snacked off plates if they left their doors open, and swam round and round Trout Lake while parks board officers shouted at her.

London paused in preparation to shake herself off. "Tsunami alert!" I yelled. We ducked, but London doused us. Then, with a farewell tail wag, she shot into the trees beside the dock.

Through the bulrushes, on the other side of the lake, we saw a parks board officer with a leash. Even from the dock, we could tell that his face was mottled with rage.

"Maybe I can catch London," said Talbot. "She's costing a fortune in fines, and both Mr. and Mrs. Butterwick are unemployed right now." He sprinted away.

That was the problem with being conscientious. At the slightest sign of a problem, Talbot felt he had to take off like Superman.

He was especially protective of London. He took her for miles-long walks, once even over the Lions Gate Bridge to Ambleside Park in West Van, where he hurled a, by now, much-chewed old baseball in the ocean for her to retrieve. Talbot was definitely a boy who needed a dog, but he couldn't have one. Mrs. St. John was allergic to dogs.

"London will be in Burnaby by the time that officer gets here," I objected, but Talbot had disappeared into the trees.

To the left of me, a blackberry bush shook.

London must've circled back there. Avoiding thorns, I pushed the brambles apart, looking for London's happy silver face with the black, liner-like tracing around her eyes that made her look so pretty.

"Good dog," I said into the blackberries. "I like you, even if you arc the 'hood headache."

On my knees, I pushed more brambles aside, and then I saw her.

Oh, not London.

Beak-Nose.

Chapter Five

The Talons of Revenge

Violet Bridey had plumped out from the wiry leanness I remembered. But her dark eyes still flashed with scorn, and the tip of her long, hooked nose still quivered. I'd always thought that its quiver, like the first trembles of an earthquake, signaled a massive inner amount of energy that could explode at any moment.

I'd been through an earthquake a few years earlier, at school. Desks rattled and papers fell off the bulletin board. Pantelli, who suffered from motion sickness, threw up into my pencil box—his, he explained after, was new.

I could handle an earthquake. I didn't know if I could handle Vi Bridey.

"We'll bypass the fact that you think my looks have gone to the dogs," she remarked in that rich, low voice I recalled from the performance she gave, at the Roundhouse Community Center downtown, of excerpts from *Macbeth*. "It's not my fault I've fattened. They serve starchy food in prison. They do that to slow you down, you know. Being bulky, you're less likely to make a break for it, they figure. Know what, though?" She leaned through the blackberry tendrils, unmindful of the thorns.

I could feel the tension coming off her in waves. "Er, no," I said, gulping. I rose—and promptly turned my left ankle because the foot was asleep and devoid of feeling. Not the greatest prelude to a speedy escape.

Beak-Nose shot a large-knuckled hand out, clamping my arm. "Chunky as I am, I still escaped. *And they won't be able to catch me.* No one can.

"Oh, don't yell," she said as I opened my mouth to do just that. "Nothing will happen to you"—she paused—"*today.* I'm quite aware that your famous vocal range could reach every person in this park. And that dark-haired boy who's so devoted to you, that Sir Galahad in scuffed Nikes, would bound back in a second."

I wrenched my arm free and glared at her. "So what do you want from me, Violet Bridey?"

She cracked the knuckles, one by one, of each hand. Her own personal drumroll. "Vengeance," Beak-Nose replied. "You can't get away with spoiling my life. Before you put the police onto me, I was headed for New York—Broadway—the big time. Well, an eye for an eye, my snoopy songbird. I'll see to it that you never make the big time either. Or *any* time, for that matter."

Beak-Nose formed her hands into claws and reached for me again.

"You nutty escaped con," I said coldly. "I'm not afraid of you."

Beak-Nose broke into a smoky laugh and withdrew those large hands. "*Bravissimo*, Dinah! Keep it up. Talent *and* gumption. I like that. *But the talons of revenge will sink into you, nonetheless."* She threw back her head to cackle at this fun image.

Beak-Nose released the brambly branches all at once, scattering blackberries on the dock. Snapping sounds ensued as she tramped past the blackberry bushes, into the trees. Her voice echoed back. "You see, I've concocted the ultimate disguise for revenge, Dinah. Better sharpen your wits...mind your p's and q's...and let the games begin!"

Her mirthful cackle faded into the trees.

Constable Fanshawe sighed. "The police are on a nationwide lookout for Violet Bridey. Now *you* claim to have seen her in Trout Lake Park, Dinah."

"I'm claiming to because I did," I said, insulted. "I'd know that beaked honker anywhere."

Loud barks outside. London zoomed past our living room window, followed by the parks board officer. "You come back here!" he shouted. "I'm going to impound you under Municipal Regulation 54-3E-28D."

London barked joyfully. To her, this was a frolicsome game of tag.

Talbot raced after the parks board officer. "C'mon, mister, I'll return the dog to her owners!"

Carl and Carlotta Featherwhist raced after Talbot. In theory I was babysitting the Singing Toddler Twins today, but they found London much more interesting than me. They yelled, "Wait for us, London Bridge!"— their witty nickname for the dog—and squealed with laughter.

Like the cars of a train, London, the parks board officer, Talbot and the Featherwhist twins veered and curved around trees. This was better than a parade. Forgetting about Beak-Nose for the moment, I twisted around on the sofa to watch through our open window.

Silver face beaming, London bounded toward me. She parked her front paws on our windowsill to smile and pant in greeting before dashing along the side of the house. Puffing, the parks board officer stumbled after her.

"London Bridge! Here, hold this for me, will ya, Dinah?" Carlotta tossed her headless Barbie doll, which she carried everywhere, through the window—where it smacked against Constable Fanshawe's left ear.

The constable gazed thoughtfully at the headless doll. Carlotta had red-magic-markered the neck with pretend bloodstains. She'd decapitated Barbie after listening to Talbot describe the death of Mary, Queen of Scots.

Constable Fanshawe murmured, "My husband's been mentioning wanting to start a family. I may tell him I prefer to put that off...possibly for years..."

There was a clang and then a loud bark.

"Oh, dear," Mother exclaimed, rising. "Jack left some garden tools propped against the side of the house. I hope no one—"

Crashes and clangs of metal hitting our cement path were followed by a heavy thump. "YEOW!!!" yelled the parks board officer.

London appeared round the front of our house again. The game of tag over, she calmly trotted home.

It occurred to me that Beak-Nose wasn't the only fugitive leading authorities in circles.

Talbot strode into the living room. "Phew!" he exclaimed. "Talk about your Olympic sprints."

Flopping into our overstuffed, cat-clawed chintz chair, he began tossing the much-chewed old baseball up and down. With a nervous glance at her nearby Royal Doulton

Bo-Peep, Mother flinched. She needn't have worried. Talbot was the best catcher and thrower in the 'hood. Surefire aim every time.

Talbot added, "By the way, Mrs. Galloway, I directed the parks board officer to the cabinet where you keep your first-aid kit. He said if you were looking for him, follow the drops of blood."

"Just a normal day here on Wisteria Drive," Mother informed Constable Fanshawe wearily. "Talbot, sooner or later London will be caught and sent to the pound. She needs more attention than the Butterwicks or you, just visiting with her, can give."

Constable Fanshawe was musing, "Mrs. Galloway, is it possible to send Dinah out of Vancouver until we recapture Violet Bridey? Not that we won't keep watch on your house and take every precaution…"

Her voice trailed off, leaving an implied *but* for lots of possibilities, all of them gruesome.

"We have relatives back east," began Mother.

"Pantelli and I will camp outside the house," Talbot announced with determination. "I'll set up a tent on the front porch, Pantelli on the deck."

"Pantelli won't be here. He's leaving for science camp," I reminded Talbot.

Talbot glowered protectively at me. Briefly I was back again on the Trout Lake dock, when he'd twined his fingers through mine and said, *You always look great to me anyway.*

…*anyway*…

And then I made a decision. I heaved a deep breath in which I relinquished, all at once, Ho Hos, Twinkies, pecan pie and all my other thousand or so favorite treats.

"I'll go to Salt Spring, to the fat farm."

"DINAH...OLYMPICS...RED-HOT...SINGING...
BLAST BRITISH COLUMBIA INTO LIVING ROOMS
AROUND THE WORLD..."

I held the telephone away from my head. Mrs.
Beechum's shrieks of delight were hurting my ears.

"EVERYONE WILL HEAR YOU...PEOPLE ON
GONDOLAS...PEOPLE ON ALPINE SKI LIFTS..."

I set the phone down on our hall table, beside the
grandfather clock. This way, the chairwoman of the Olympics
promotional committee could rant as long as she wanted.

Madge came up beside me. In her white tennis
halter-top and skirt, she was cool and fresh, even *after*
her tennis game. "You're going to the fat farm after all?"
she demanded.

"PEOPLE AT CAFÉS ON THE CHAMPS
ÉLYSÉES..."

"Yeah, well." I fiddled with the hem of my L-sized
T-shirt. "I decided maybe it was time I stopped being
a chubbette."

Madge knelt beside me. She was so *very* pretty.
I doubted Madge had ever had an un-slim moment in her
life. My own life was fraught with them.

"You *could* eat better than you do," she said, scanning
my face. "So the fat-farm thing might work out. As long as
you're not going there because of some dumb body-image
anxiety attack or anything like that."

"Easy for *you* to talk about body image," I mumbled.

I thought Madge would object to that remark, that
she would slough off the idea of her beauty the way figure
skaters slough off their spins and leaps when you tell them
how clumsy *you* are by comparison. But Madge was cool
in more than body temperature. She was too smart to
pretend the obvious wasn't true.

She tipped my chin up so that I had to look at her. "Do you know what happens when you and I meet other people for the first time?"

I tried to twist my chin out of her hand, but she wouldn't let go.

"They gape at me," Madge continued calmly. "They gawk. Sometimes they even coo. *But that's for the first few minutes.* Do you know what happens after that?"

She let go of my chin. But I kept looking at her.

"They notice *you*," Madge said. "If there's a piano or a guitar or, hey, even some forks and glasses in the room, they beg you to sing. They're entranced by your voice, Dinah-Mite. And they're riveted by your energy and humor, because, being you, you bounce around and wisecrack. You're fun. You make people feel good."

I grunted. I hadn't thought of it that way. I grunted again, to show that she'd got through to me. I'm into meaningful emoting.

Madge smiled. "Do you know what I love about Jack? He's that rare male who was interested enough to find out what was going on behind the outside me. With him, I'm not a"—she grimaced—"trophy, to be shown off, like I was to other guys. Remember Roderick?"

I shuddered. Roderick was the dweeb Madge went out with before I introduced her to Jack, at the time of my spy in the alley mystery.

Slowly we grinned at each other. Madge said, "Lose some weight, but not a lot, Dinah. Promise? For one thing, I have a feeling you're due for a growth spurt, and you'll need some of that chubbette flesh to accommodate it."

"PEOPLE IN THE PAMPLONA BULL RUN..." came a shriek from the phone, and we both jumped.

"What, exactly, made you decide to go to the fat—the fitness retreat?" Madge inquired.

"Well…you," I replied. "Saying you had to let out my bridesmaid's dress. But not just you. Talbot. He told me he liked me anyway, chubbette or no.

"I don't want to be an *anyway*, Madge. Not to him. Not to anyone."

Eventually I got a comb and scratched it against the receiver. "Bad connection, Mrs. Beechum," I shouted and hung up.

The phone promptly rang again. "Yeah, I know," I sighed into it. "People will hear me on the steppes of Russia."

"Dinah?" came Angela's shy, hesitant voice.

"Er—hi, Angela." I adjusted my voice, trying to sound as friendly as possible, since she and I were about to spend a month together *chez* fat farm. Mother was pleased. She thought it would be, quote, "a nice chance" for me to get to know a girl, since I only ever hung out with boys.

"I just heard that you'll be at the health and fitness retreat," Angela ventured. "I'm really glad."

"'Really glad'?" I repeated. I supposed this was how girls talked. Icky and sweet. I rolled my eyes. "Let's see now. Okay, I'm *levitating* with joy."

"Though that horrid Cornwall's going too," Angela was lamenting.

The one, albeit tiny, bright spot was that the fitness retreat's owner, Mrs. Cuthbert, had sounded cheery and friendly on the phone. And that Pantelli, at his camp on Mayne Island, would be a short ferry ride from Salt Spring.

Which reminded me. "You know my friend Pantelli?" I asked. "He wanted to know if you had an e-mail address he could write you at."

"Pantelli…the tree boy?"

"Yeah," I said brightly. Pantelli had begged me to put in a good word for him with Angela. I struggled and then came up with, "But there's more to Pantelli than just *trees*, Angela."

I lapsed into silence. Hopefully Angela wouldn't ask me to elaborate.

Then I heard Angela's mom in the background. "Who are you talking to, Angela? I thought I told you *no more phone calls*."

"Wow, what a suspicious maternal unit," I remarked. Maybe not the most tactful comment, but then tact isn't my strong point. In fact, with me it hardly qualifies even as a weak point.

"It'll be good to escape Mother for a while," Angela murmured sadly and hung up.

Dot Bridey sure is controlling, I thought.

And I decided there were worse circumstances than being a chubbette.

Chapter Six

Welcome–sort of–to Salt Spring

It turned out that Talbot packed his bags before I did. With me heading off to the fitness retreat, and London fated to be impounded any day, his parents decided he needed a distraction. So they were sending him to science camp with Pantelli.

Mrs. Featherwhist brought Carl and Carlotta over for a final babysit before I left. Talbot, dogsitting London, joined us.

"LONDON BRIDGE!" the twins shrieked and enveloped London in hugs. In response, she let out a cheerful series of rising-up-the-scale barks.

A parks board van pulled up in front of the Butterwicks'. The officer, arms and legs bandaged from his encounter with our gardening tools, limped up the Butterwicks' steps.

Talbot shook his head. "Sooner or later he'll catch London off-leash. The Butterwicks are so busy hunting for work they don't have time to exercise her. They just let her out in the back lane. Which London interprets as a launching pad."

He sighed. "If only London hadn't zoomed in the back door of Cobs Bread last week. She cleaned the place out—giving fresh meaning to the term 'loaf around.' Complaints bombarded the parks board."

Getting no answer at the Butterwicks', the parks board officer hobbled back down the steps. He noticed London, narrowed his eyes and gave her a mean, I'll-get-you-my-pretty gaze. Then he roared off in his van.

Talbot mourned, "And once London *is* captured, the Butterwicks won't be able to afford the fee to spring her." He stared hard at the ground, and I knew he couldn't bring himself to add the possible finale to London's prospects. If unadopted, she'd have to be put to sleep. The *big* sleep.

On Salt Spring Island, Mother swung onto Tripp Road, which dipped down to St. Mary Lake. We squinted at addresses painted on leaning mailboxes or on crooked boards nailed to trees. "So rustic," Mother breathed. This was the sort of thing she found charming. "And all these blackberries and blueberries growing wild, Dinah!"

"As long as the place has cable," I said grimly.

I had more or less fortified myself in the backseat with PlayStation and suitcase on one side, and dozens of CDs, my portable player and a pile of graphic novels on the other. My *Judy Garland at Carnegie Hall* poster was rolled up in a special packing tube that I held on my lap. The closer we got to the fat farm, the harder I pretended the tube was Merlin's wand, which I could wave and in an instant make this whole experience disappear.

Mother had kept asking if I *really* wanted to go, up to and even during the ferry ride from Tsawwassen, south of Vancouver. I didn't want to go, no, especially as Madge, Jack, Talbot, Pantelli and Wilfred the Cat slipped farther and farther away from view out the back window. And as visions of celery sticks danced in my head.

But to beg off would be to backtrack. Something I, Dinah Galloway, was too stubborn to do.

"Here we are," Mother said. She turned the car onto a pebble drive with apple and plum branches hanging so low they scraped the top of the car. Then the branches slid away and we saw a large, green, ranch-style house surrounded by blackberry bushes. An old van was parked in the carport beside stacks of firewood.

We pulled up by the rust-colored front door. It was divided in half, an old-fashioned, country style that prompted a "Charming!" out of Mother. The door's lower half, decorated with an iron rooster, was shut. Through the upper half, which was open, a slim, gray-haired woman smiled at us while drying a plate with a dishtowel.

"No dishwasher," I commented to Mother in the car. "Ergo, the cable prospects are doubtful. How backward *is* this place?" I pretended to peer past the woman. "Why... at a primitive table, someone's working on blueprints. The title is—can I make it out? Could it be? Yes. 'Plan for a new device: *the wheel.*'"

"Dinah, please! How embarrassing if she hears you." Mother flashed a nervous smile through our open windows at the woman. "That must be Mrs. Cuthbert, the owner."

Mrs. Cuthbert, in a faded denim shirt and jeans, pushed open the half door and took long, athletic strides toward us. She was lean, with tanned, leathery skin and sprigs of hair escaping from a bronze clip.

"So good to meet you, Mrs. Galloway," she exclaimed, giving Mother's hand a vigorous shake that caught her off balance. "And Dinah—it's an honor. I've heard songs from the *Moonstone* CD played on the radio." Her gray eyes took on a faraway look. "You know, when you sing, I think I'm young again."

Now how could I dislike anyone who said that? "I'm glad," I mumbled and allowed my own hand to be throttled by her shake.

Then Mrs. Cuthbert surveyed the contents of the backseat. "You're like that other famous redhead, Queen Elizabeth the First," she observed. "You travel with a large retinue!"

I adjusted my glasses and viewed her with friendliness. This woman had promise. "Did you know that Queen Elizabeth *ordered somebody's hands chopped off*? Some guy who'd published some pamphlets criticizing her. He wasn't discouraged, though. He raised the bloody stumps and—"

"Dinah has a friend who tells her about history," Mother interrupted quickly as Mrs. Cuthbert paled. "Its more ghoulish aspects. Talbot's such a nice boy otherwise," Mother added, puzzled.

"Well, you won't be needing these things," Mrs. Cuthbert said firmly. She stuffed the PlayStation, CDs and graphic novels deeper into the backseat. "You will be *outside*, exercising and playing sports, Dinah. In the evening you'll be far too tired to read"—she picked up a stray graphic novel that had slid from her grasp—"*Joey the Homicidal Android*."

"Not my Joeys," I objected in alarm. Pantelli, Talbot and I were co-buying the Joey series and sharing them around. We'd formed our own book club; we had reports and discussions. Watch out, Oprah.

Mother persuaded Mrs. Cuthbert to let me keep the Joeys. And, most importantly, the *Judy at Carnegie Hall* poster. I'd had it since kindergarten, a gift from Dad in the days when I still called Carnegie Hall *Crumbly* Hall. Shrugging, Mrs. Cuthbert gathered up all my bags and led us inside. We had to break into a run to keep up with her long strides.

"Angela's room is across the hall," explained Mrs. Cuthbert, "and Cornwall will be staying over there." She pointed out my window to a silver trailer parked behind the carport. "Mrs. Blutz insisted he have his own quarters, equipped with pure, self-circulating air."

I envied Cornwall. Imagine having your own digs!

I leaned my elbows on the windowsill and looked down the yard. Way down. It was a huge property with, I thought glumly, lots of room for running and other athletic pursuits. Halfway down to the lake, the yellow grass sloped to several archery targets. Cornwall and Angela were aiming arrows at them. Cornwall was at least hitting the edge of targets; Angela was missing them altogether.

Angela set down her bow. Wrinkling her nose, she exclaimed, "Archery! *Ewwww.*"

I started laughing—until a look from Mother silenced me. "*Right,*" I said. "I'm supposed to study and adapt to this new, strange species, the adolescent female."

"On your mark, get set, GO!" Mrs. Cuthbert shouted.

She, Cornwall and Angela took off round the large—the *very* large—track field near the top of Tripp Road.

About ten yards along, Mrs. Cuthbert stopped, her baggy, blue silk track shorts fluttering around her lean legs. "Dinah?" she called back to me in a not overly patient inquiry. The others kept going, Cornwall in a heavy, lumbering jog; Angela in a dainty, tiptoey one.

"I didn't want to embarrass you guys by easily overtaking you," I explained.

"*Move* it."

The problem was, there wasn't just an *it* to move. There was a *them*: all the chubbette folds from all the extra eating I'd done in my twelve and two-thirds years. The folds bounced and waggled as I ran. Cornwall, glancing back, noticed and pointed, hooting.

I plowed, gasping, along the sandy track. "How… much…longer?"

"Dinah, you've only gone five steps," Mrs. Cuthbert informed me unsympathetically.

Cornwall and Angela were halfway round by now. I collapsed on the grass beside the track. "Couldn't I just be pleasingly plump for the rest of my life?" I pleaded.

Mrs. Cuthbert sat down gracefully beside me. Shoulders back, she crossed her legs and folded her feet up on top of her knees. I knew this was called lotus position. Madge sometimes did it as part of a de-stress meditation exercise. I would've needed a crane to get one of *my* feet atop a knee.

"Sure, you can give up on athletics," Mrs. Cuthbert said. "And a healthy diet? Toss that out too while you're at it."

"Good." I flopped backward and studied the sky, which was a flawless blue. Now this was *my* kind of outdoor activity. Madge liked quoting the late artist Yves Klein, who said blue was the color of infinity. I was with

Yves on this one. I could watch the sky forever, on and on, melting into the horizon…

"It's fine for you *now*, Dinah," said the fitness expert's dry voice, off to my left, like a buzzing mosquito I couldn't ignore. "You're young. The bad habits you're indulging in now won't boomerang on you till middle age, when a glaze of grease encases your heart like a jellyfish. When gallstones form and block your body's ducts."

I started quacking at her, wit that I am.

"Ducts meaning *passages*," Mrs. Cuthbert elaborated, frowning.

The woman had no mercy. She continued, "When fat turns your liver into a gray, useless glob. When the part below your esophagus, which is the tube from throat to tummy, can't close properly, and your semi-digested food jumps back up into your throat. That's a charming problem called acid reflux. Remember the fairy tale about the girl who spewed out toads every time she opened her mouth? I've often wondered if the author of that story wasn't using the toads as a metaphor for acid re—"

"NOOOO!" I yelled. Cornwall and Angela, three-quarters of the way round, stopped to goggle across the grass at us.

"Please," I begged Mrs. Cuthbert and struggled to my feet. "I can take the gross stuff, but when you introduce *metaphors*—and on my summer vacation!"

I decided the only way to shut Mrs. Cuthbert up was to start jogging around the track with her. I didn't go quietly, though. I heaved my breath in and out in ragged moans. I wailed. When a couple bicycled past us, I mused loudly about what the phone number for reporting child abuse might be.

When I was finally silenced to catch a proper breath, Mrs. Cuthbert inquired, "All that, er, 'gross stuff' I was telling you about, Dinah. Did that have no impact on you at all?"

I paused to wipe my foggy glasses on my T-shirt. "Of course it did," I said impatiently. "But I filed it away. I always do with scary stuff. I know I'll have nightmares about it, so why waste the daytime?"

"Do you have a lot of nightmares, Dinah?"

"Yeah, tons. Really impressive ones too. Better than Joey the Homicidal Android at his blood-dripping best. About my dad crashing his car into a tree and dying. About this dude on a cruise ship who tried to drown me. Lately about…"

I stared round at the trees bordering the field. It was a quiet moment, with no cars passing on the road above; all we could hear were the leaves whispering. And I got that feeling again, that someone was watching me. I squinted. That shadow behind the far oak *could* be a figure; that flash of light in the leaves, a face.

I shook the feeling off. Like I say, why bother? I'd experience it again soon enough, in 3-D, more-vivid-than-life, Technicolor nightmares.

I breathed out heavily and laced my voice with sarcasm. "Let me guess, Mrs. Cuthbert. Your not-too-subtle questions about nightmares…part of the whole fat-farm experience, I take it, is head examining." I pushed my hair back and cocked an ear. "There. Examine. File a report."

To my surprise, the fitness instructor called my bluff and peered inside. "Ah," she said. "You know what I see?"

"Ear-wax buildup?"

"A strobe-lit stage surrounded by darkness. On the stage, a feisty redhead performing her heart out. And…"

"Please. I'm breathless with suspense."

"She's afraid to get off the stage," Mrs. Cuthbert finished gently. "Afraid to go out in the darkness."

Chapter Seven

Strict Rules, By Gum

The round, green, Ping Pong-sized balls glistened at me in their coating of light, low-cal margarine. I glared back. In a face-off with Brussels sprouts, I was determined not to flinch.

"Fine," said Mrs. Cuthbert, and she spooned the Brussels sprouts off my plate, onto hers.

She then passed round a bowl of roasted slivered almonds for Angela and Cornwall to scatter over *their* Brussels sprouts.

My stomach, unsatisfied with the smallish sole filet I'd been given, rumbled in protest. You can't want Brussels sprouts, I told it. You *can't*. Have some pride.

Angela refused to try archery anymore, so I took my stand beside Cornwall. *Whish!* My arrow hit the third black ring from the middle.

Cornwall actually had the technique—gracefully drawn-back fingers tightening over the shaft—but I had the animal energy. Red-faced and sweaty, Cornwall collapsed on the grass. "Where does a tub like you get your strength?" he gasped.

"I'm not a tub," I defended myself. "I'm charmingly rounded."

Later I mulled over his question. True, I had lots of energy. However, now that I thought about it, my endurance probably had more to do with the breathing exercises my singing instructor taught me. I might not have the discipline to stick with other things, like diets and regular homework times, but I was serious about my singing. I practiced heaving my breath in, holding it and heaving it out again every day, twice a day, for ten minutes. If I was waiting somewhere, in the dentist's reception area or for a bus, I practiced then too. The odd looks I got didn't bother me—I *liked* being the center of attention.

And I figured that, one day, all this practicing, even the radio-commercial gigs singing about Sol's salami, would lead to Crumbly—I mean Carnegie Hall. Like Judy!

"Zing went the strings of my HEEEAAARRRT," I belted out, just as Judy had done that memorable night in 1961, when she restored her reputation from a has-been to a forever-will-be. Nobody's ever sung like that, before or since.

I rummaged in my suitcase for the blue tacking clay Mother had given me to avoid marking Mrs. Cuthbert's wall with thumbtack holes. Ah, here it was, under the carefully folded shorts, shirts and jeans I had no intention of unpacking. I mean, I was only here for a *month*.

As I was carefully sticking up my poster, I heard a timid voice behind me. "Is Judy Garland your idol?" Angela asked.

"For her singing and her guts, yeah," I returned. "Not for her lifestyle choices so much. She got screwed up with drugs and alcohol. But she never *gave* up."

"I'd love to hear a Judy Garland CD some time," Angela said wistfully. "At home I'm only allowed to listen to opera. If I'm to succeed as an opera singer, I can't listen to anything else, Mommy says. Once she caught me listening to Jack FM and screamed her head off."

"Poor you," I said bluntly. "Beak-Nose for an aunt, and the Wicked Witch of the West for a mom! I know. Let's chew our woes away."

I flopped down on the bed and offered Angela some bubblegum from the large, multi-flavor-filled plastic bucket Talbot and Pantelli had presented to me as a going-away gift. They figured gum would be okay on a fat farm.

"Watermelon flavor's good. Take five pieces," I urged Angela. "Quantity's important. I figure gum's not worth it unless you can blow bubbles that guarantee liftoff."

Mrs. Cuthbert loomed in the doorway. "Do I smell sugar?" she said ominously.

We watched Mrs. Cuthbert pour the gum, piece by delicious, wrapped piece, into the large drawer of a beige metal filing cabinet. I was unable to suppress moans of dismay as I viewed the goodies already in there: Crispy Crunch bars, Kit Kats, Oh Henry! bars…Glimpsing a Cadbury Caramilk, I almost wept. The only science I've ever been interested in is how they get the caramel syrup inside those chocolate squares.

"You're not the first Cuthbert's Fitness Retreat client to bring an illegal substance onto my property,"

Mrs. Cuthbert said briskly. "At least you were open about it, Dinah. I've had young clients smuggle treats in by stitching them inside jacket linings. One boy emptied Smarties into an umbrella. Unluckily for him, it rained one day, and I grabbed the umbrella. Quite a pitter-patter the Smarties made as they bounced off my doorstep!"

At the memory, the fitness expert gave a low, malevolent chuckle. To me, though, her story was a Shakespearean-level tragedy. All those Smarties, wasted!

"I only brought gum," I objected.

"Not *sugarless* gum," Mrs. Cuthbert pointed out, wagging her finger as if I were a witness she was demolishing on the stand. She finished pouring the gum pieces; the last to tumble in was my favorite flavor, banana and honey.

Mrs. Cuthbert snapped the drawer shut, locked it and dropped the key into her shirt pocket. "I give out all these candies on Halloween to neighbors' children. Yes," she added, smiling at our glum faces, "once a year I do share the sugar around. Everyone should have one unhealthy day per three hundred and sixty-five."

She handed me back the empty plastic bucket. I placed it on my head. Might as well put it to *some* use.

For dinner we had salad, lean roast beef, a tiny amount of mashed potatoes and a lot of broccoli.

"Dinah just emptied her broccoli into her napkin," Cornwall tattled. His pale, turnip-like face broadened with a nasty "gotcha" grin.

"Is this true, Dinah?" Mrs. Cuthbert demanded.

"Um." I clamped down on an impulse to hurl the broccoli at Cornwall. Instead, plastering on a wide, toothy and very fake smile, I spread my white napkin and broccoli chunks on the table. "I'm creating installation art," I explained. "Evergreens on an Arctic meadow."

Angela broke into a grin and quickly ducked her head low over her plate. Mrs. Cuthbert's face, however, was icy. "I operate Cuthbert's Fitness Retreat on a three-strikes basis, Dinah. The gum and the broccoli add up to two. One more, and you're out. You pack your bags, and I drive you to the ferry."

"Fine." But it wasn't fine. It was mega-unfair. I hadn't known gum was "illegal." Meanwhile, the smirking Cornwall had got away with snitching—the lowest and slimiest of crimes.

I adjusted the bubblegum bucket more firmly on my head. Then, not taking my eyes off Mrs. Cuthbert, I crammed the broccoli into my mouth, all at once, every bit of it.

After dinner, Mrs. Cuthbert showed us a tall bookcase crammed with games. She suggested—translation: ordered—that we hang out in the living room and play checkers or cards, or put puzzles together.

Ix-nay on videos and computer or video games. She explained, "These tend to make you withdraw into yourself. To be unsociable—and being unsociable generally means being inactive. I want you to be *extroverts* here. To draw yourself out of yourself. To think of yourself as part of a team, working together to improve your health and everyone else's. Oh, and Dinah? If you keep rolling your eyeballs like that, they'll unhinge from their sockets."

With a vague smile, she walked outside, sat down on the deck and assumed the lotus position. And then she chanted, "Om...om..." Mrs. Cuthbert was into meditation;

she said it soothed her. I'd noticed she was increasing her meditation times of late.

I couldn't imagine feeling team-like with Cornwall. In fact, I was plotting one of my BBIS (i.e., Blazingly Brilliant Ideas) as payback to Corny for tattling. Maybe I'd shove him in the lake. Or pull his trailer door slightly ajar and prop an open can of pink paint on it.

For now, though, Angela and I sat down to play checkers while Cornwall emptied puzzle pieces out on a coffee table. Angela, I noticed, was looking slightly less pale here at Cuthbert's Witless Retreat. Maybe the fresh air was perking her up. Or maybe it was being away from her controlling maternal unit.

"Is that a pop-can ring you're wearing?" Angela inquired shyly as I jumped one of her checkers.

We were on our fifth game. Angela, I thought, privately, was too nice for any sort of competitive challenge. She always lost. I had the feeling she thought jumping an opponent's checkers would be rude.

I was wearing the pop-can ring Talbot had given me on a black cord around my neck. "Oh, that," I said, embarrassed. "That's a…um…a—"

"Gift from a guy?" Angela asked and smiled. "I bet it's that cute guy who was at your house. Not the tree one," she added with emphasis.

Poor Pantelli! And here he had a crush on Angela.

Angela got up to scan Mrs. Cuthbert's bookshelves. The fitness expert had apparently kept a lot of her childhood favorites: there were Archie comics and classics like *Treasure Island*, and then a bunch of *Girl Athletes' Annuals*. Angela withdrew an annual with a cover of some smiling tween tennis players hammering a ball over a net.

Talk about your objectionable content. I shuddered.

With a good-night wave, Angela retired to her room.

I realized it was nine o'clock, bedtime *chez* Cuthbert's Fitness Retreat. I gave Angela a wan smile in return because I was suffering homesickness pangs for my buddies.

In my room, I got into bed, opened the window wide because it was so hot, and tried to sleep.

Beyond my door, rumbling noises began.

A minor earthquake? I scooted into the hall. A rectangle of light glowed at the end: Mrs. Cuthbert, paying her bills by lamplight, at the dining room table.

The rumbling rolled through Angela's door. I stood, listening. She was snoring! I choked back a laugh. For such a pale, quiet little thing by day, she sure was a rip-snorter by night.

I returned to my own bed and tried to escape to the land of Zs.

And couldn't.

And still couldn't.

At home I'd be buttering a mega-bowlful of fresh popcorn and settling in for Leno or Letterman. Mother had given up trying to get me to bed early years ago. In contrast to her and Madge, I was a night owl, like my late dad.

I prepared to flop over for about the hundredth time. Heck, I'd soon burn off the ten pounds through sleep deprivation.

I was used to Angela's snoring by now, but a new sound joined it. From the deck, sudden and piercing—a cackle. I froze in mid-flop.

Someone, or something, was right outside my window.

Chapter Eight

Only the Beak Knows...

A hook-shaped shadow was inked against my window screen. Because the milky beams of the full moon backlit the shadow, I couldn't make out a face. Or, for that matter, any limbs.

I stayed statue-still. I didn't think the shadowy visitor could see my face either; my bed was to one side of the window, out of the moonbeams' path. I decided to hold off on a good, blood-curdling scream and see what the visitor would do. Maybe it would creep in, and I could surprise it with a hearty bash from the bedside lamp.

The shadow pressed close to the screen. "Hee, hee, hee!"

Beak-Nose! I remembered that cackle from the Livingston Theater, where she'd tried to swipe the valuable moonstone.

I broke out in a sweat that would've sent Noah to the shipbuilder's. I inched my hand toward the lamp. It was about time somebody straightened out Violet Bridey's nose for her.

"Hee hee!" Cackling, the shadow withdrew across the deck. I sat up and pressed my nose against the screen. Actress that she was, Beak-Nose glided slowly, dramatically through the strobe-like moonbeams. Past the hot tub, she shrank into a smaller and smaller inkblot until she blended in with the large shadow cast by Cornwall's trailer.

I zoomed out of my room, down the long hall and past Mrs. Cuthbert doing her accounts at the dining room table. "Beak-Nose sighting!" I yelled and shoved aside the sliding doors to the deck.

Outside, I came up short against the night's total stillness. The moon lit up Cornwall's trailer with an unearthly glow; this made the shadows around it all the darker. "She's hiding behind the trailer," I whispered.

"Are you sure there's someone there?" Mrs. Cuthbert questioned doubtfully. "Did she say anything?"

"No, she just cackled. That's her MO."

"Stay here," the fitness expert ordered. She went inside, turned on the deck light. I twitched with impatience. The moon was illumination enough, and Beak-Nose was probably slipping away.

We prowled around the trailer and then the carport. No one in sight. The yard was also lit up almost all the way to the road.

"She's hiding somewhere," I said.

"Dinah, we'd be hearing yelps of pain if she were. My property is bordered on both sides with blackberry bushes."

We heard the trailer door open. There was a *clunk*, an outraged yell and a series of clatters.

Cornwall appeared around the corner. He had his arms extended, with hands hanging limply off them, like

Frankenstein's monster. Only Cornwall looked way worse than the monster ever did.

He was slathered head-to-toe in maple syrup.

"I left the door to my trailer open because it's so hot tonight," Cornwall related to Constable Leary. "Somebody must've balanced a can on top of the door while I was sleeping. When Loudmouth over there"—a maple-syrupy forefinger jabbed in my direction—"woke me up, I pushed the door wider to go outside and investigate. *Wham*. The can emptied on me and crashed down the trailer steps."

"Beak-Nose," I said grimly. "She's our night stalker."

Constable Leary was a kindly faced, slim man whose bed-head hair showed he'd been sleeping peacefully until our call. He, Mrs. Cuthbert, Angela and Cornwall all blinked blearily at me. We were in the dining room; Mrs. Cuthbert had swathed Cornwall's chair in bath towels before he sat down.

"There've been no reports of Violet Bridey arriving on Salt Spring," the constable said. "And we've watched for her at all ferry terminals."

"Besides, why would Violet Bridey play pranks on Cornwall?" Mrs. Cuthbert demanded. "And that maple-syrup can came from my storeroom," she added, annoyed.

"We all know you're the one who did it, Dinah," Cornwall accused.

"I—" It occurred to me that the maple-syrup-can idea was awfully close to the pink-paint-can one I'd had earlier. Did I have the makings of a criminal mind? I gulped.

At my hesitation, the others frowned, their suspicions hardening. "Wait a minute," I said. "You could've set *yourself* up, Cornwall. You heard Mrs. Cuthbert give me the three-strikes warning." I stood and glared at him. "With me out of the way, you'd get to do the Olympics commercial."

Cornwall rose too—and took all the bath towels with him. He tried shaking them free; no luck. They were stuck fast.

"Maybe you should have a quick swim," Angela suggested timidly. "That'd wash the syrup off."

Cornwall tried breathing angrily in and out through his nostrils—but they were stuck fast too. Exploding in a cough, he stormed out of the room, too indignant to speak.

Or, I thought, too guilty to speak. Maybe I'd got it right. Maybe he *was* trying to frame me.

At breakfast, Cornwall glared at me over his muesli. I tried to lighten things up by asking if he had any leftover maple syrup I could add to my own muesli. That got a ringing silence, though Angela did smile into her bowl.

Which she ended up not able to finish. "A bigger breakfast than I normally have," she apologized.

With difficulty I mustered my pride and didn't beg, sobbing, for her leftovers. I was *starving*. Breakfast, without a minimum three poached eggs?

After breakfast, Mrs. Cuthbert spent a long time on the phone. From the deck, where Cornwall, Angela and I were doing the push-ups she'd assigned, I caught muttered snippets. "So difficult, Mrs. Beechum." "Bright, yes, but extremely uncooperative." And "First time I've thought about giving up on someone."

Mrs. Beechum must've convinced her to stick it out

with me, because Mrs. Cuthbert emerged looking tight-lipped and dissatisfied.

Again, I tried to lighten the mood. "Imagine saying Angela's difficult!" I joked.

Again, a ringing silence. With Mrs. Cuthbert stiffly disapproving of me, and Cornwall not speaking to me at all, the atmosphere was cold enough to store ice cream in. I pretended not to be bothered, but I was. Sometimes I think I act so outrageous, peppering every statement with wisecracks, to hide just how much things *do* bother me.

I wouldn't have made it through the next days without Angela. If she hadn't been there, with her shy friendliness, I'm positive I would've hiked to Long Harbour and hopped the ferry home.

Instead, she and I became buddies. Yeah, that's right. I, Dinah Galloway, developed a friendship with a *female*. Unprecedented for me.

With Angela, I learned you could have fun in a quiet kind of way, taking walks or playing cards or checkers or treading water in St. Mary Lake and chatting. You didn't have to hang upside down from trees while bellowing joyfully at the discovery of an intriguing set of leaf stria, like Pantelli. Or deafen the neighborhood for blocks around with exuberant guitar playing, like Talbot.

With Angela, I didn't even mind "sharing," as she termed it. Normally I would've made barfing noises at the idea of trading feelings about stuff.

As we leisurely breaststroked across the lake, Angela confided in me about her problem with snoring. On the previous year's class trip to Ottawa, the girls she roomed with had mocked her mercilessly. "Snore like a boar! Angela *Boar*dey!" The other kids took it up too, even on a tour of the Parliament Buildings. "*Snore like a boar, Boardey!*" A couple of Mounties, explaining that Parliament was in session and the class was being disruptive, marched the lot of them outside.

"Crowds of other tourists stared at me," Angela sighed.

"Whoa! Talk about your silver linings," I commented.

We reached the middle of the lake, and I stopped to tread water. Jack had taught me to swim last May, in the swimming pool aboard the cruise ship *Empress Marie*. He'd probably saved my life in the process, given that a villainous passenger had a penchant for tossing me into deep water.

I shuddered at the memory. Angela thought I was shuddering in sympathy with her. "It was horrible, Dinah. I was so *humiliated*. Mother flew out and took me home."

The sun bathed my upturned face. I shut my eyes. Jack was right about the sheer restfulness of treading water. I considered what I would have done in Angela's place. Tackled the ringleader with a headbutt? Naw. I was into flair, not violence. Smashed several Ho Hos into the ringleader's face? Eaten the Ho Hos, more likely. Sent phony e-love-notes from the ringleader to the creepiest boy in the class? Ah, yes. Now *that* was a top-rank BBI.

I bit back a chortle. Somehow I didn't think this was the sort of feminine "sharing" Angela would appreciate. Instead I did the sidestroke and looked at the property across the lake. It was huge and heavily forested. The couple who owned it, nature lovers, camped out when they stayed there, Mrs. Cuthbert had told us. But this summer they were in Europe.

"I have huge tonsils, that's why I snore so deafeningly," Angela explained. "They push the muscles at the back of my throat up, partly blocking the air passages. My snores are the noise the air makes as it tries to move back and forth."

"Well, snore away," I said graciously. "I don't mind. I *like* loudness."

There was a lot of exercise, yes, but I grudgingly realized Mrs. Cuthbert was more interested in keeping us active than torturing us. She let us walk fast around the track field rather than jog. She let us splash around in the lake rather than ordering us to do laps or anything grisly like that. She let us punch a volleyball around rather than battle over points. She encouraged us to shoot arrows just to build up arm muscles rather than worry about hitting bull's eyes. Good thing, because Angela, try as she might, unfailingly shot wide.

Physical education, Mrs. Cuthbert maintained, had got a bad name because kids associated it with punishment. "Activity should be spontaneous," she said one day over a lunch of whole-grain bread with mayo, tomatoes and avocados. "Activity should be something you feel comfortable with. Maybe once in a while you decide to exert yourself with a bit more of it than usual. The operative words are, *you decide*."

"Ah, free will," I said and gulped back some bottled water. Needless to say, there was nary a pop can to be found on the Cuthbert premises. "Father Claudio taught us all about free will. The first time he mentioned it, I thought he wanted us to spring a guy named Will from jail."

Angela giggled, Cornwall stayed stonily silent— but Mrs. Cuthbert's weathered face lapsed into a very faint smile. You'd almost need a microscope to detect it, but it was there. "Always the wisecracks, Dinah," she commented.

I decided to try widening her smile. "Here's a non-wisecrack, Mrs. C. I've been sleeping. Loggishly. From nine thirty p.m. on, as compared to from one a.m. on at home. All this activity must be draining my energy."

"Well, it'd be impossible to do that," the fitness expert said, but not crossly. "You can thank the exercise—and the fact that you're not snacking after dinner. In the evening, our bodies are pleading for sleep. Sugar from evening snacks jumpstarts them."

Angela and Cornwall left the table while I collected dishes. Every day we took turns. Mrs. Cuthbert asked in a low voice, "And no more Beak-Nose visits?"

"I don't *think* so," I said. "But then, I'm so tired she could be staring through my window from dusk to dawn for all I know." I didn't add that, despite the heat, I now shut and locked my window every night.

I stared over the stack of dishes at Mrs. Cuthbert. "You do believe that I saw her, don't you? Honestly, I don't make stuff up."

"Well." Mrs. Cuthbert mulled it over. "I've come to know you better, Dinah. Your perception of the world is so vivid that you don't *need* to make things up." Then she relaxed and at last gave me a genuine, fourteen-carat smile. "I believe that you *think* Beak-Nose was there. And maybe you didn't prop the maple-syrup can over Cornwall's door. I can't imagine who did, though."

Cornwall, obviously, I wanted to say, but on a rare diplomatic impulse decided not to annoy her when our tattered relationship was finally mending. I staggered off with the plates, wondering if Mrs. Cuthbert could be right—if I had imagined the Beak-Nose sighting. It could've been a dream, I supposed.

A dream equipped with surround sound, I thought, remembering the cackles.

With no PlayStation and computer games, I was fast becoming a checkers demon. Later that evening, I fingered a piece, considering the board. The trick, I was finding, was to look ahead and second-guess what might happen.

"Aha," I said, hunching my shoulders and rubbing my hands together in my best evil-scientist imitation. I grasped the piece and, *slap, slap*, I triple-jumped Angela. She smiled and shrugged at yet another defeat.

"Your problem is, you're too polite," I advised her. "You're always trying to please others. You have to be tough, Angela. Don't worry about offending people."

"But, Dinah, I was *raised* on worry," Angela said ruefully. With her slim, tapered fingers she tidily emptied the pieces back into the box, folded up the board and cracked open another *Girl Athletes' Annual*. She was on her way to reading through the whole series.

Everything Angela did was quiet and graceful—the opposite of me, I thought in chagrin. "On the other hand, I wouldn't mind offending people a *little* less frequently," I sighed.

Cornwall, slumped over a jigsaw puzzle, sneered, "Shed any ounces yet, Tubs?"

This was, in fact, a source of concern for me. Besides being snack deprived, I hadn't exercised so much in my life. I *must* be shedding. I had this vision of wandering around Salt Spring dropping clumps of fat, an excess-weight version of Johnny Appleseed.

I could only guess at any weight loss, however. Mrs. Cuthbert didn't own a scale. She thought that obsessing about pounds distracted from the whole point of fitness. Come to think of it, this was pretty much Madge's philosophy too.

"You're not exactly buff, buddy," I informed the stocky Cornwall.

Cornwall snarled at me and went outside to his trailer. After a minute I heard him talking to himself in a loud voice. "It's a universal adolescent feeling, trying to find your place. The adolescent who is perfectly adjusted to his environment I've yet to meet. Go, Cornwall. *Go*."

My eyebrows ascended to the vicinity of the North Pole. Cornwall was giving himself pep talks? I snorted. Of *course* we adolescents weren't "perfectly adjusted." That was the whole beauty of the age, in my view.

The next day Mrs. Cuthbert decided to take Cornwall, Angela and me into Ganges. While she shopped, we'd be allowed a—gasp!—treat of our choice in an Internet café. Yes, *Internet*. We'd also be allowed to check our e-mails.

"In other words, we'll have a gloriously unhealthy hour," I cheered as I washed the lunch dishes.

Then Cornwall informed me with a snigger, "You'll never make it, Tubs. We're biking."

Biking? As in, up *hills*? Salt Spring had too many of those for comfort. Why couldn't the Olympics promotional committee have chosen a fitness place on the nice flat prairies?

Despite my horror, I mustered a comeback. "So…we're *chatting*, Cornwall? I should've checked my horoscope today: ugly developments will occur."

But Cornwall had just as much trouble as I did with the hills. He and I had to dismount and walk our bikes up a couple of the larger ones. Stung by his "Tubs" jeers, I taunted him every second of the way; Mrs. Cuthbert was safely out of hearing range, ahead on the road with Angela.

I homed in on the book he had in his bike basket: *Roger Bannister, Unlikely Hero of the 1954 Commonwealth Games*.

I hooted. "*Bannister*, huh? What'd he contribute to the Olympics, some stairs? What's next, Edward *Ladder*? Emily *Footstool*?"

Yet again I was appreciating the value of my breathing exercises. Though my legs were achy from pedaling, my lungs were fine and fit for nonstop lame jokes.

Cornwall was turning the shade of uncooked hamburger meat.

We reached the top of the last big hill, and I was able to sail ahead with Angela into Ganges. I noticed Mrs. Cuthbert had to hang back with Corny. His uncooked-meat hue hadn't gone away, and she was hovering concernedly over him.

"He might be having an asthma attack," Angela said.

"Good," I said. I knew I was being mean, but I didn't care. I couldn't forgive Cornwall for calling me Tubs. I just couldn't. All the noise I made, singing and otherwise, was my act of faith in life, my way of trying to be part of it, to make it better. To have someone ignore all my trying and insult my appearance, my eating problem—okay, I admitted it, I had one—was like a slap. Like a *We don't need or want you*.

Like a judgment that the total of everything I ever was and tried to be added up to just so much fat.

Chapter Nine

Exercise? Try Exorcist

Still lagging back with Cornwall, Mrs. Cuthbert waved us on ahead into the Salt Spring Roasting Company Café. Angela and I locked our bikes to a rack and, feeling pretty roasted ourselves in the hot sun, fled gratefully under the striped awning.

At the counter, goodies stretched before us. Fat muffins bursting with chocolate chips or blueberries or cranberries; croissants glistening with chocolate swizzles; playground-sized brownies. Okay, that last was a bit of an exaggeration, but after almost a week of being sugar-free, I couldn't be rational. "Brownies," I moaned. "My long-lost friends…"

I armed myself with one, plus a giant steamed milk, and plunked in front of a computer. Ditto Angela. We both logged into our e-mail accounts.

The Internet on my computer took longer to chug on, so, unabashedly curious creature that I am, I glanced over at Angela's e-mail. At a message from DotBridey@telus.net.

The audition tapes you prepared for your opera coach were brilliant: bell-clear, beautifully edited. You have so much talent, Angie. Always keep your mind on your career. I know how easy it would be to get distracted at Mrs. Cuthbert's, with that lively, mischievous Dinah Galloway around. But please, don't be unproductive. Concentrate on your career, Angie, your career!

What? I thought, offended. Me, an unproductive influence?

With a *tsk*, Angela deleted the message. I looked away, face burning.

I checked my own messages. Worried ones from Mother and Madge inquired if I needed anything, i.e., to be brought home. And urged me to mind my manners, of course.

I thought about what I might need: barrels of Smarties were out, so I asked instead for them to send me some oil paints. *Lots of 'em. Glow-in-the-dark ones. I might take up nighttime painting*, I wrote. I thought some more and added, *In the spirit of Cuthbert's Fitness Retreat, better include lots of paint* thinner.

Having dazzled the Galloway women with my humor, I skipped to the messages from Talbot and Pantelli.

First message, from Talbot, the day I left:

Hey, Dinah. I miss you already. And on your behalf, I'm freaked about The Beak. Just be careful, okay? E me if anything weird happens. About a stranger showing up at the fitness retreat, say. Or about anything at all out of the ordinary. No matter how minor. E me if, I dunno, your toothbrush is missing a bristle. I'm serious, Di. A slight change in what's around you can mean a lot. Take Emperor Augustus Caesar, who noticed his fig tree was gleaming brighter than usual in the sun—only he didn't pay attention. And look what happened. I told you about him, right?

Yeah, you did, I thought. But I couldn't remember what Talbot had said. For the moment, with fearful thoughts of Beak-Nose buzzing in my brain, I couldn't give a fig for Augustus Caesar and his problems. I read on.

So puh-leeze. PAY ATTENTION to stuff. The smallest thing could be a tip-off that she's near. Cuz, remember, Vi Bridey isn't just The Beak. She's Super Beak. Nobody seems able to stop her. They sure can't catch her. Anyhow, gotta go. I'll e you again super soon.

All of a sudden the brownie tasted way too sweet. I could hardly get it down. Beak-Nose, on the prowl for revenge—no wonder everybody was so anxious about me.

I clicked on Pantelli's message.

Science camp rocks, Dinah. Today we visited this Japanese garden. Lots of Japanese cherry trees! I took over from the tour guide and gave everyone a lengthy lecture on aphid prevention. Japanese cherry trees are particularly vulnerable to aphids, I explained.

Giving the lecture was so much fun I asked about coming back for another tour. The guide suggested September. Too bad, cuz she'll have returned to the University of British Columbia by then.

Tal was on the tour but didn't pay much attention to my aphid talk. He was busy yakking it up with this nice girl named Shandi. For the past few days the two of 'em have been inseparable. Like two seeds in a yellow wood pod. BTW, the yellow wood, an east coast tree, is endangered. Interested in contributing to the Save the Yellow Wood Fund? The Junior Dendrologists' Association is working to—

I clicked off the rest of the message. Not that I wasn't sympathetic to the yellow wood, but I was wondering who this Shandi was. What kind of name was Shandi, anyway? I thought crossly. And who did she think she was, distracting Talbot from sending me e-mail messages?

And Talbot. Some fair-weather friend *he* was. Not that I minded, nooooo.

I minded so little that I bashed rather than clicked open Pantelli's next message.

This one bore an attachment. *Hey, show this to Angela, will ya? It's a special treat. I'd have e'd it to her directly, but I don't have her address.*

I leaned around the side of the computer to where Angela was googling places to buy hair ribbons in Ganges. (Girls!) "Pantelli sent you something," I said, not without uneasiness. The last attachment he'd winged my way was a trailer for the remake of *Texas Chainsaw Massacre*. On the other hand, a Pantelli attachment could equally likely be a short documentary on trees. With Pantelli you could count on either being frightened senseless or bored to sleep.

"Sure," Angela returned.

Opening the attachment, I let Angela have my seat and watched over her shoulder.

Pantelli had sent us a slide show called "Find the Dot." It started out with cute, sappy photos of the sort that make a lot of the e-mail rounds: babies, kittens, flowers, hummingbirds. As each photo came up, Angela had to find the dot and click on it; that brought the next photo to the screen. Yech, I thought as a toddler with an adorable smile popped up. Pantelli's taste had gone way downhill.

A photo of a—yup, I'd guessed it—hummingbird came up. Sunshine dotted the pretty photo. So *many* dots to choose from this time. Angela clicked on one; nothing happened. Then another. Nothing. Then—

Wham. A photo of a decomposing female head popped up, its greenish-hued white skin peeling off, teeth rotting, eyes chillingly blank. *SURPRISE!* read the caption.

I recognized the photo: Linda Blair in *The Exorcist*. I leaned back and laughed loudly. Good old Pantelli! And here I thought he'd lost his touch.

Angela leaned back too, but out of fright. Her eyes were bulging. "How...horrible," she breathed.

Uh-oh, I thought. Girl alert. Swallowing more hearty laughs, I assured her, "That's Pantelli's way of showing he *likes* you."

"Oh." Angela hurriedly pressed the space bar, which brought the slide show back to the first shot, of some cheery yellow chrysanthemums. Then, with an effort, she made herself grin. "I think...maybe...your friend Pantelli gets *ahead* of himself sometimes."

I gaped at Angela; then I grinned back. "You made a funny! And a warped one." I shook her hand. "Way to go. Angela, you're a mensch."

I'd learned the word *mensch* from Sol of Sol's Salami, the place I did radio commercials for. "A good egg," I elaborated, at Angela's puzzled expression. "A peach."

I shrugged, unable to come up with any other synonyms. Food ones were the type I tended to, especially now, when I was food deprived.

But Angela's grin grew wider. She'd got the message. "Pantelli likes me, huh?" Angela mused, as if such an idea might not be *quite* as horrible as the decomposed-head shot. "Hmmm..."

By the time Mrs. Cuthbert walked into the café with Cornwall, we were giggling girlishly. At this rate I'd soon be into sewing and baking.

The ghoulishness and giggles had swatted away

thoughts of Beak-Nose and restored my appetite. After all, this was a rare unhealthy-food afternoon here on Salt Spring. I'd better make the most of it. I stuffed the rest of my brownie back all at once and greeted Mrs. C. and Corny with a chocolaty-toothed smile.

Mrs. Cuthbert ushered the still-flushed Cornwall over to us. His eyes and nose were streaming. "Poor Cornwall had an asthma attack from pedaling so hard," Mrs. Cuthbert said, her voice quivering. "Thank goodness I remembered to carry his inhaler in my knapsack.

"Oh, Corny," she mourned, hugging him. "I feel so responsible. I shouldn't have pushed you to exert yourself. From now on, I'll only ask you to do low-stress exercises, and then only if you feel up to them."

Cornwall grabbed the napkin I'd had my brownie on. He blew his nose and wiped his eyes.

And, over the napkin, slid me a sly look. "That's okay, Mrs. Cuthbert," he said. "If I don't feel well, I can always watch Dinah exercise."

"I'm heavily into punching," I fumed back. Then, as Mrs. Cuthbert looked inquiringly at me, I quickly added, "Bags."

"Why, what a nice photo," Mrs. Cuthbert exclaimed about the yellow chrysanthemums. She sat down in the chair Angela had vacated. "Is this your picture, Dinah? It's lovely!"

"It's part of a slide show," I said, glowering at Cornwall.

"One of those soothing, meditative ones, I bet." The fitness expert gave me a grateful smile. "Do you mind if I watch the slide show? Something meditative is just what I need to lift my spirits." Grasping the mouse, she pressed the first dot.

In my dismay, I forgot all about being angry with Cornwall. "Er, no, Mrs. Cuthbert, I don't think you'd find this very medit—"

"Sssshhh, Dinah. I'm *enjoying* this."

"But—"

"It's so calming. So relaxing." Mrs. Cuthbert pressed the dot that led to the hummingbird surrounded by sunshine.

Moments later, as the fitness expert's screams filled the Salt Spring Roasting Company Café, I realized that the goodwill I'd tried to rebuild with her was now totally demolished...

"Honestly, I do *try* to fit in," I agonized to Angela.

We were trudging along a trail in a gully in Mount Maxwell Provincial Park. Vine-wrapped branches drooped over our heads, as if struggling to reach the almost-dried-out stream beside us. Tree roots knuckled out of the dark, cracked soil. The shade was more suffocating than refreshing. The whole of British Columbia was now hotter than hot; we were probably breaking drought records back to the Pleistocene era.

Far behind us, Mrs. Cuthbert proceeded at a slow pace with Cornwall. They were taking frequent rest and water stops, which put me in the unusual position of being at the head of an athletic outing.

Though the word *head* was a sore point with me right now. If only Mrs. Cuthbert hadn't clicked through to the gruesome finale of Pantelli's slide show!

"But no matter how hard I try, I still come across as outrageous and offensive," I continued lamenting to Angela.

I wondered if Shandi was quiet and demure. I supposed so. I'd sneaked onto Mrs. Cuthbert's laptop the night before and checked my e-mail. There was a message from Pantelli expounding some more on the yellow wood, and the usual love-you-miss-you-be-good message from Mother.

But zilch from Talbot. His interest in me, it seemed, was going the way of the yellow wood. Extinction.

"You just have a lot of energy, Dinah," Angela said. "*I* think most people adore you for the way you are. However, because you're such an in-the-face type, there's always going to be a minority of people who find you..." She hesitated tactfully.

"Annoying? Obnoxious?"

"A minority of people who don't understand you," Angela amended. She glanced back at Mrs. Cuthbert and Cornwall, seated on a log. Mrs. C. was pouring trail mix into his open palms. The type with chocolate, I bet, I thought to myself, seething.

Cornwall sent a smirk our way. He then said something whiny to Mrs. C. I was sure I caught the word *Dinah*.

Angela said wryly, "And sometimes they're a rather *vocal* minority."

We looked at each other and burst out laughing. Hey, there was something to this female sharing stuff. And Angela was living proof that quiet plus well-behaved does not equal dull. I decided then and there to put more Angela into my personality. To become the new, improved Dinah and leave the old, immature one behind.

We trudged to the top of a trail, out of the shaded part—and reached a vast, gorgeous meadow. Here the heat became a gift: the sun's shimmering waves heightened into the richness of wet paint the blue of the scalloped camas flower, the snow white of the Easter lily, the rich cocoa of the chocolate lily. These and more flowers, as well as shrubs of delicate white snowberry and sparkling green rock moss, were scattered like brilliant gemstones over the pale grass. At the opposite edge of the meadow, against some Douglas firs, a stag paused in nibbling some oat grass, surveyed us calmly and then went on snacking.

I was recognizing the different plants, not due to any naturalist inclinations on my part, but thanks to Madge. She'd painted nature scenes on a visit to Salt Spring a couple of summers earlier and rhapsodized about them on her return home. This meadow was part of the rare Garry oak ecosystem, she'd told Mother and me. "The artist Emily Carr said, 'In all your thinkings you could picture nothing more beautiful than our lily field.'"

I'd scoffed at Madge's enthusiasm, but now I totally got it. What a drool-worthy place!

"I'll take your picture," Angela offered when I told her about Madge. "You can e-mail it to your sister."

"Okeydokey." Handing her my camera, I positioned myself in the middle of a wildflower patch, stretched my arms wide and put on the special, ghastly, fake smile—eyes popping, teeth bared—I reserved for photographs. I was pretending to be Julie Andrews in the opening shot of *The Sound of Music*. Angela backed under the shade of a Garry oak at the edge of the meadow and snapped the photo.

Then I sprinted over to snap one of her. As I focused, she leaned against the oak, her hand toying with the dainty velvet hair ribbons she wore.

There was a rustle of leaves overhead. I was too busy bashing at the temporarily jammed camera button to pay attention. "You just have to get tough with these gizmos," I explained to Angela. "I recently got our TV remote working again this way. Somehow I jammed the channels, but why would anyone want to switch away from Turner Classic Movies, as I pointed out to Mother. So many good gangster flicks…"

I had the camera working, but Angela wasn't looking at me. She'd backed up against the tree trunk to gaze through its rustling leaves to the mountain slope beyond. She was so pale, paler even than usual, that her eyes bulged out in contrast like licorice gumballs.

Finally I realized what was wrong with this picture, so to speak. *Rustling* leaves—in a breezeless drought?

"MOVE, DINAH!" screamed Angela, and she jumped forward to shove me on the ground…

Just as a giant rock plummeted to smash her on the head.

Chapter Ten

The Mysterious Madame Sosostris

The woman with the plump, painted, papier-mâché hens smiled at me. "Are you lost?" she asked sympathetically. "The Salt Spring market is so sprawling—so many twists and turns."

I looked back, past the throngs of marketgoers admiring jewelry or wood sculptures, or sniffing at exotic spices, or spreading umpteen toppings of jam on huge, hot rounds of bread. Mrs. Cuthbert and Cornwall were studying some paintings of local scenery and wildlife.

"I *feel* lost," I admitted to the woman with the hens. "I don't know anything anymore."

I chose a red-polka-dot-on-white hen for Mother. "A friend of mine got hit by a falling rock yesterday, and now she's at Mrs. Cuthbert's, resting, on doctor's orders." Feeling close to tears, I chomped my lower lip. "And she was the only friend I had around here too."

"Oh dear," the woman clucked, much like a real hen.

She bundled the red-polka-dot hen up in lots of sparkly, star-decorated tissue paper.

"The rock grazed the back of her head, as opposed to thumping it squarely on top. The doctor says those few inches of difference made the accident an injury as opposed to a fatality.

"But I don't think it *was* an accident," I said. "I think Beak—I think someone threw the rock down the mountain slope, intending it for *my* skull, not Angela's."

From the display of paintings, Mrs. Cuthbert glanced past the milling crowd, checking on me. She was worried and drawn. Everyone else—doctor, police—thought the falling rock had been an accident. In this drought, the soil had dried up so much that rocks were loosening from slopes. I insisted otherwise, which meant that once more I was Mrs. Cuthbert's problem guest.

"Oh dear," the hen woman said again. She was the plump, comforting type, with short brown hair and glasses that flashed in the sun like beacons.

At the moment my vision of the beacons was blurring. "You mustn't cry," the hen woman clucked. She pressed the wrapped-up hen into my hands and patted my shoulder comfortingly.

"Angela pushed me out of the way," I said. "I think she saw someone throwing the rock. But now she's too weak and too medicated to remember. Her mother's with her, and the doctor. They won't let me question her. Mrs. Cuthbert says if I do, I'll have to go home."

My tears plopped on the tissue paper. At one point the day before, in exasperation, Mrs. Cuthbert had demanded, "Why can't you *cooperate*, Dinah? Beak-Nose hasn't been seen anywhere on Salt Spring. It's hard enough dealing with what's happened to Angela without your imaginings."

I tore off some tissue paper to wipe at my eyes. I heaved a big shaky breath and managed a wan smile back at the kindly hen woman.

We were attracting glances. Passersby glanced from teary me to the hen woman, lifted their eyebrows and shied away from the hen stall.

"Here," the hen woman said, hurriedly placing a wrapped peppermint stick on top of the hen. "There's nothing like a bit of sugar to take the sting out of life."

I regarded the peppermint stick wistfully. The old Dinah would've ripped off the plastic wrapping and vacuumed up the candy. The new, improved Dinah was conscientious, like Angela. The new, improved Dinah obeyed rules. No sweets for me.

I handed the peppermint stick back to the hen woman, who was busy conferring in the shade of the tree behind her stall with a slight, slim man swathed in scarves. "That's fine, thanks, I don't need one," she told the man, who was darkly tanned, with bottle-bottom sunglasses and huge white teeth. Shrugging, he flapped an enormous yellow scarf at her and disappeared into the shade.

"Who does he think he's kidding?" The hen woman chuckled. "I've seen those scarves for sale at the dime store!"

She took the peppermint stick back from me, peeled the plastic off and chomped the end of the stick. Between noisy chews, she suggested, "Why don't you go see Madame Sosostris, the fortune-teller? Yes, what a good idea," the hen woman urged, noticing some new customers. "Off you go then, poppet. Madame Sosostris will cheer you up. Quite a character, she is!"

Madame Sosostris? Vaguely I recalled that name from somewhere. But I wasn't in the mood for horoscopes.

The way my week was going, they'd probably turn out to be *horror*scopes, in any case. I explained, "Actually, I don't want—"

But the hen woman shooed me down the next row of stalls. I was sorry to leave the cheerful fat hens, glowing in their flaming shades and patterns of red.

"Scarves, missy?" barked a hoarse voice. The scarf man jumped out at me from between a baking and a tatting stall. He flapped the yellow scarf in my face. In the sunlight, both his teeth and the scarf were blinding. I brushed past him.

"Candles?" A long-haired woman thrust a lavender-scented candle at me. She'd lit it to accentuate the scent.

I shook my head and kept trudging. I had no particular plans. No particular friends, either. I was becoming Ms. Unpopularity with a growing segment of the world's population.

"Shandi," I muttered. "What kind of name is *that?*"

"Whoa!" shouted the scarf man. I glanced back. The long-haired vendor's outstretched lit candle had set fire to one of his scarves. Passersby squirted the contents of their water bottles over him. That was the advantage of this hot weather: everybody but everybody was armed with water.

I took a chug from my own bottle. I had to admit, once you got used to it, water was the number-one refreshing drink. Even more so, surprisingly, than coconut-flavored root beer.

I trudged down the next row, past stalls with stickily scrumptious, candy-stuffed nougat; salsa in tongue-burningly delicious flavors from green curry to roasted pepper; cookies, cakes and brownies brimming with rich, smooth fudge, with calories so exorbitant they'd be beyond numerical ranking, in infinity.

Just my luck to end up in a food row, I reflected sourly—and then I reached a stall draped with purple curtains from whose gauzy materials gold and silver stars winked and shone. A sign overhead read *MADAME SOSOSTRIS, FORTUNE-TELLING. $5.*

Protruding between the curtains, on a snowy-tablecloth-covered table, was a huge crystal ball. Ghostly shadows floated around inside it. I bent to look at one, but it turned sideways and glided round the circumference.

"It's your shadow, hon!" cackled a skinny old woman layered in purple shawls. "Hee hee hee! The crystals in the ball are refracted, warped, so every shadow that falls in on them whirls out of shape. Much like the future, doncha know. We think we can outguess our fate, but the stars are too wily. Nothing is as it seems, hee hee!"

She pushed her long, straggly gray hair aside and leered. I stared back at her.

Specifically, at her beak nose.

It was massive, like a ski jump, and dotted with two enormous moles.

I tried to wrench my gaze away from it. "You must be Madame So-slalom—I mean Sosostris," I said, gulping.

"You betcha!" the fortune-teller cackled.

Violet Bridey cackled too. I backed up a step. Aside from the nose, Madame Sosostris didn't look like Vi Bridey. On the other hand, Vi *had* promised the ultimate disguise. The moles could be false.

Madame Sosostris dipped her beak nose at me. Her narrow eyes glittered. "Come with me into my magic stall, and I'll tell your future with my crystal ball!" She waved her hands around wildly.

They were bony hands, like Violet Bridey's. That did it.

I wouldn't make a scene, though. Being the new, improved Dinah, I'd handle this quietly.

"All right," I murmured to Madame Sosostris. "The jig's up. I'm making a citizen's arrest."

The fortune-teller froze her waving hands in midair. "Whaddya mean, *arrest*? I got my license to be here."

"Let's file out of here in a calm, orderly manner to the police station," I said. Not that I knew where the police station actually was. Memo to self: check on law-enforcement locations *before* booking people.

Madame Sosostris scowled. "Looky here, who sentcha to pester me? Was it Madame Stargazer? I tell ya, it's dog-eat-dog in the fortune-telling biz these days. Shoo! Off with ya!"

Dang it. I'd have to resort to the wig test. I reached and tugged.

"YEOWWWW!" The fortune-teller staggered back. She clutched her scalp.

Marketgoers and stall owners alike rushed up to us. "What a nasty girl," exclaimed the woman selling chocolate fudge. "Poor Madame Sosostris, getting attacked!"

"And she has so *little* hair left too. Imagine someone yanking at it," tut-tutted the candle seller, in an overwhelming rush of scent.

"Maybe the kid didn't like the fortune Madame told her," Scarf Man cracked hoarsely.

"You be quiet," the hen woman scolded him. She hugged the moaning Madame Sosostris. "I'm sorry, Velma. And here I'd sent a nice young lady to be cheered up with one of your optimistic predictions. Wonder what happened to her."

"I don't know..." Madame Sosostris was turning pale. The rocking, obviously intended to be comforting, was rather vigorous. "If you don't mind, I'd prefer to remain stationary..."

Being short has its advantages. Neither Madame nor the hen woman could see me in the crowd of people anxiously pressing around them. They'd become quite the attraction at the market today; I felt a clap on my arm as someone shoved me aside for a better look.

A note of suspicion sharpened Madame's voice. "You said you sent 'a young lady' to me? Was she redheaded?"

Mother's boyfriend Jon, who directed me in *The Moonstone* last fall, taught me never to miss a cue. I wasn't going to start now. This was exit time if there ever was one. Hunching, I crawled past people's legs to the table. Lifting the white tablecloth, I slipped under.

On the other side, I emerged in Madame Sosostris's curtain-swathed stall, with fortune-telling books stacked on one side, and a CD player and speakers arranged on the other. High-pitched flute music piped out. I guessed this helped get Velma into the witching mood or whatever.

I stepped to the other side of the stall, parted the starry, purple gauze curtains and found myself in the middle of a lineup for a Mexican restaurant.

"No cutting in," someone objected, but a nicer someone else glowed at me. "How positive of you, to be carrying around such hopeful messages!"

"Uh," I said. Then I realized she was staring at my arm. At a neon green sticky note that had been attached there.

I remembered being clapped on the arm just before I'd slipped into the stall. I peeled the sticky off. There was a message scrawled in capital letters:

NO MATTER HOW BAD THINGS SEEM, YOU DO HAVE A PAL ON SALT SPRING.

"You've made my day, dear," the nice someone sighed happily.

I flipped the sticky over. There were more words on the other side. Definitely not the day-making kind.

What happened to Angela was meant for you. WATCH OUT.

Chapter Eleven

Chilling Howls

The doctor said all Angela needed to do was stay on the pills he'd left and sleep, sleep, sleep. Which she was doing—but Dot Bridey still wouldn't relax. She was going through boxfuls of tissues, either crying into each one or tearing it into shreds out of jitteriness. I almost made a joke about investing in Kleenex stocks but controlled myself. I was being the new, improved Dinah.

Instead I tried a Brussels sprout. It actually wasn't bad. I speared another one. Okay, one more, but that's it, I told myself. After all, I had principles.

Crunching on the slivered almonds that came with it, I tried to summon thoughts of the gooey desserts I'd gorge on, once I was sprung from Cuthbert's Fitness Retreat. But all I could think of were the fruit trees outside Mrs. Cuthbert's house: the tart plums, sweet blackberries, tangy apples. Mrs. Cuthbert let us eat as many as we wanted.

I realized that, deprived of Ho Hos and other old

faves, I was redefining what *sweet* meant to me: all natural, all healthy.

Could this mean the end of Ho Hos in my life? Were Ho Hos and I *breaking up?*

Talk about your shattered love affairs.

My sad musings were interrupted by snores roaring down the hallway from Angela's room. This happened every once in a while, making Mrs. Cuthbert jump and Cornwall sneer. Dot Bridey would massage her forehead.

I didn't mind the ripsnorting. After all, Angela didn't snore nonstop. Only when she turned on her back, she'd explained to me.

And Angela was my buddy. If she hadn't pushed me aside, I'd be the one under medication. Or, if the rock had hit me squarely on the head, under embalming fluid.

Remembering how mean Angela's classmates had been—*Snore like a boar, Boardey!*—I scowled at Cornwall until he stopped sneering.

With a surly shrug, he piled the dishes into a tower-high stack. Wobbling under the china's weight, Cornwall staggered with weaving steps into the kitchen. The dishes swayed dangerously. If I hadn't disliked Cornwall, I would've laughed. This was the type of thing Pantelli would do as a way of scaring his mother into never asking him to clean up the dishes again.

Instead I pondered who the author of the sticky note might be. The hen woman, I thought. She'd been awfully nice—awfully pal-like.

But why would the hen woman take an interest in me?

And why had she sent me to Madame Sosostris?

Madame Sosostris. I knew where I'd heard that name before. From Mother!

I started to rush for the phone. Then the new, improved Dinah took over, and I politely asked if I might use it.

"Of course, dear," Mrs. Cuthbert replied, looking surprised and pleased.

Her pleasure didn't last long. There was a long, loud series of splintering-china crashes from the kitchen.

Cornwall hadn't *quite* made it to the sink.

"Madame so *what*? Dinah, I can hardly hear you," Mother protested.

"That racket you hear," I replied, enjoying myself hugely, "is Cornwall trying to get out of being blamed for breaking most of Mrs. Cuthbert's china. He's claiming it happened because of his asthma, but she's not"— I winced as Mrs. Cuthbert's voice rose to shrieking pitch— "buying it."

There were also the background chinks and crackles of Dot Bridey sweeping up the broken dishware. I took the phone into the living room and tried again.

"Madame Sosostris, Mother. I know you've mentioned her name in your quotations."

"Oh, *that* Madame! She's in T.S. Eliot's poem *The Waste Land*. She's a fortune-teller who sees without seeing, if you understand what I mean. Quite a common theme of Eliot's actually. He—"

"Mother, my youth is draining away…"

"Sorry, dear. Very well then. This is what Madame Sosostris says:

And here is the one-eyed merchant, and this card,
Which is blank, is something he carries on his back
Which I am forbidden to see.
Does that help?"

"Not really." Somebody with one eye was carrying a blank card on his back?

"I'll have to think about this," I said. The Salt Spring market's Madame Sosostris had two eyes, at any rate. As well as a slalom nose weighed down with huge moles. I shuddered.

"Dinah, are you sure you don't want to come home? Mrs. Cuthbert let us know about Angela's accident. She thought you might be too upset to stay on."

She *hoped* I might, I thought sourly. Mother's voice was so loving, so trusting compared to Mrs. Cuthbert's, that I almost weakened. How tempting to hop on the next ferry and be with Mother, Madge, Jack and Wilfred within a few hours. To stretch out on my bed, snuggle Wilfred and look out over the peaked rooftops of our Grandview neighborhood to the row of blue Coast Mountains, familiar and reassuring as childhood buddies. To feel safe—and appreciated.

"It was a mistake to send you away," Mother fretted on. "Talbot's mom feels the same about him. The first day at science camp, she phoned Talbot. He was utterly miserable, she says. He couldn't stop worrying about you being threatened by Beak-Nose, and the Butterwicks' dog being threatened by the city pound. Such a conscientious boy."

"I'm sure *Shandi* thinks so."

"Who, dear?"

"Oh, nothing." Talbot *was* conscientious. That was the odd thing. He'd promised to e-mail me. It wasn't like him not to follow up, even if this Shandi was the ultimate distracting tween fatale of all time.

"Dinah? Do you want to come home?"

"Um…" I stepped out on the deck and considered. Yes, of course I wanted to. But Angela had got bashed in the head on my behalf. And we were becoming friends, which meant a lot to her. To me too, I realized. I had an actual *girl*-friend. Wow.

Reluctantly I said, "Naw, I'll stick with Cuthbert's Witless—I mean Fitness Retreat till the month is up, Mother."

A few moments later I switched off the phone and—being the new, improved Dinah—was about to head back into the kitchen to help clean up.

It was then that a strange, piercing howl echoed around our end of St. Mary Lake...

Mrs. Cuthbert, Cornwall and I stood peering round the lake for the source of the howl. Dot Bridey had stayed back to sit with Angela, in case she woke at the sound of the howl and got upset. Though from the way Angela's mom kept twisting her long hands and breaking out in polka dots of perspiration, I would've said she, not the howler, was more likely to upset Angela.

We surveyed the swamp, the various canoers and kayakers skimming the length of St. Mary Lake, and the deserted ranch across from us.

Or *was* the ranch deserted? Not a dry leaf or blade of grass budged in this heavy heat—but just for a moment, beyond the ranch dock, I thought I saw an evergreen twitch.

I raised the binoculars a great-aunt had sent me one Christmas for bird-watching. More interested in mysteries than feathers, I tended to use the binoculars for sleuthing. I focused on the evergreen. A thick piney branch still trembled. There *had* been someone there. Or something.

"Maybe the howl came from a werewolf." Cornwall shivered.

"Afraid?" I jeered.

"Aren't you?" he snapped back.

A large V-shaped ripple sped by. A beaver. Its big white teeth shone, reminding me of Scarf Man's chompers. Those had been unnaturally big, I thought. Whoa. Maybe *he* was Beak-Nose.

And I'd yanked at poor Madame Sosostris's hair! "What an idiot," I mumbled.

"There's nothing idiotic about Cornwall feeling uneasy," Mrs. Cuthbert scolded, misunderstanding me. She hugged him. "Either that howl came from some very mixed-up ducks or we've got ourselves an Elvis Presley impersonator somewhere on St. Mary Lake."

At night I'd continued to keep the window shut, the curtains drawn. Nervous about a repeat visit by the Night Stalker, I roasted my way to sleep.

Tonight, though, I let the cool air pour through the screen. I'd resolved to sit under the window and wait for Beak-Nose. No matter what Constable Leary and Mrs. Cuthbert said, I was sure Beak-Nose was the stalker. Who else would prowl around at midnight? Well, aside from our friendly neighborhood howling werewolf.

Also, I'd thought a lot about what Mrs. Cuthbert had said to me. About how I was afraid of what the darkness might hold. Tonight I'd decided to face up to it.

Madame Sosostris floated toward me, clutching a blank card. "Whoooo?" she demanded. "I can't see whooooo."

I sat up abruptly enough to give myself whiplash. I'd been dreaming—and somewhere outside an owl was hooting.

The drumbeat of Angela's snoring filled the house. I straightened out a crick in my neck and thought of Cole Porter's song "Night and Day." My dad crooned it to me while bouncing me on his knee. *Like the beat, beat, beat of the tom-tom, when the jungle shadows fall…*

I blinked my sore, sleep-deprived eyes, and now it was Dad, not Madame Sosostris, in front of me. His black eyes snapped with love and energy; his grin encouraged me with a warmth I couldn't get enough of, even in a hot spell.

Angela's snores throbbed through the wall…

Like the tick tick tock of the stately clock, Dad crooned from "Night and Day."

"Night and Day"? I greeted him. *Other kids would get "Rock-a-bye Baby," Dad.*

Other kids aren't you, Dinah-Mite. You'll sing at Crumbly Hall one day—

Please, Dad. I'm not little anymore. Carnegie Hall.

But you gotta get past the Night Stalker first. She's a doozy, Dinah. Mired in her own dark, brooding envy. But overconfident, I sense. Your challenge—

My Olympic challenge? I thought that was to lose ten pounds.

What, we didn't raise you properly? Never interrupt a ghost, Dinah-Mite. Now listen up. Your challenge will be to understand the stalker before she realizes you can.

BEFORE SHE REALIZES YOU CAN, Dad repeated in a loud, urgent whisper.

Or was that a loud sigh escaping someone short of breath, someone gliding across the grass? My throat closed down. I waited, huddled and still.

And a hook-shaped shadow spilled across the deck.

Chapter Twelve

The Fine Art of Weaponry

I had to make my move quickly. Grabbing the three tubes of glow-in-the-dark oil paints Madge had sent me, I squirted them out the window at the Night Stalker. (I'd omitted explaining to Madge the real reason I'd wanted the paints: self-defense.) Lunging, I striped them up and down the folds of the stalker's voluminous cloak. I grabbed the hood and squirted up into the dark depths. I tried to yank the hood off, but gloved fingers clung to it, holding it down. I clawed at the figure's other hand and pried the glove off—only to have sharp nails rake my arms.

Ah. These nails would be the "talons" Beak-Nose had threatened me with at Trout Lake. I turned my yelp of pain into the war cry Pantelli had uttered when swinging his feet toward Beak-Nose. Or, rather, the person he *thought* was Beak-Nose, Dot Bridey. "SUPER BEAK!" I yelled, and I squirted the remains of the tubes into the hood again.

Beak-Nose staggered back, bracing herself on the covered hot tub to avoid falling. She plunged down the deck stairs. The yellow glove print she'd left on the hot-tub cover gleamed luridly in the moonlight.

I vaulted over the windowsill and plunged after Beak-Nose. Forget the new, improved Dinah; this was the old, reckless one. I was seeing red—a brighter red than any oil paint.

Beak-Nose was weaving clumsily over the grass as if she couldn't tell where she was going. I must've zinged some paint in her eyes. I was gaining on her. "This is GOTCHA time, Beak-Nose!"

The shadowy hook figure stopped on the grass, whipped round. "Hee hee hee, Dinah Galloway," it hissed. A paint-splattered, cloaked arm lifted. From the cloak's folds, a knife hurtled straight at me. I dove for the ground, spraining my shoulder in the process. The knife jabbed into the soil and waved back and forth, gleaming in the moonlight.

Beak-Nose stumbled down the hill with that strange crooked gait of hers and disappeared in the shadows near the boardwalk to the dock. Her cackles echoed back to me.

"Yeah?" I shouted in frustration. "Well, she who cackles last, cackles best, Beak-Nose!"

Light fanned over the grass: Cornwall, opening his trailer door. He blinked sleepily at me.

"Beak-Nose paid another Night Stalker visit," I informed him. "Not that anyone will believe me."

Cornwall stepped out. I noticed he was wearing pj's decorated with Olympic torches and red-lettered 2010s. I was about to jeer at him—our standard mode of communication—when he said, solemnly and without any malice at all, "I believe you."

I stared, sure he was setting me up for some kind of insult. But he went on, just as solemn and a bit frightened, "I saw your stalker. And I saw you crash on your shoulder. That musta hurt, Dinah."

"Don't you mean, 'That musta hurt, *Tubs*'?" I inquired bitterly. I started for the house.

"I have a bag of frozen peas in my freezer," Cornwall offered. "Maybe we should put that on your shoulder. Hang on." He went inside.

I was too surprised by his friendliness to object. When he emerged, we sat on the trailer steps and I pressed the bag to my shoulder. The cold numbed the pain away.

"So what was all that commotion about?" Cornwall asked. "Other than the fact that you're more nocturnal than a bat."

I giggled. "It only seems that way, Cornwall. I stayed up tonight because I had a bbi. Blazingly Brilliant Idea," I explained. "I figured that if I could slather permanent, glow-in-the-dark paint over Beak-Nose, she'd be discouraged from more stalker visits. Plus, there's the purely petty satisfaction of knowing she'll spend hours scrubbing that paint off her face and hair."

I glanced back at the yellow glove print glowing on the hot-tub cover. "Beak-Nose will also need new gloves," I added with satisfaction. "In fact, her whole stalker wardrobe pretty much needs replenishing."

"Beak-Nose might have more than one cloak," Cornwall pointed out.

"*Please*," I begged him. "No logic. Mind you, I always tell my friends that, and do they listen? Nooooo."

"Your friends," Cornwall said, sounding shy. "That'd be the two guys who were at your house?"

The way he said *friends,* he sounded like an alien trying out a new word. I wondered if Cornwall's overbearing mom allowed him much time between practicing and auditions for any friends of his own.

"Yeah." I nodded. "My friends Talbot and Pantelli. And…maybe Cornwall?"

Cornwall studied his hands. I saw that he bit his nails down to the nub just like I did. And here I'd thought we had nothing in common.

He said awkwardly, "I'm sorry I called you Tubs, Dinah. And I'm sorry about the other stuff I said. I guess I was being a pretty poor sport about your getting the 2010 Olympics singing job. To put it mildly."

I shrugged. "The singing job's conditional on my losing a walloping ten pounds. And," I sighed, "I doubt Mrs. Cuthbert's planning a favorable report on me to the committee, given everything that's happened."

"Wrong-o," Cornwall said. In his certainty, he forgot to be shy and looked at me. "You *will* get the job, Dinah. The committee's not going to turn you down over a few pounds here or there."

"More here than there," I said regretfully.

"Seriously, Dinah. You have more than a great singing voice. You've got—I dunno, this appeal for people, in spite of the trouble you cause. Or, who knows, maybe because of it. Not many people can resist it. *I* can't, and I don't even like you. Or so I thought."

"Ditto," I said. I raised my uninjured arm and gave Cornwall a friendly punch in the shoulder. "By the way, I'm impressed by how you exaggerate your asthma to Mrs. Cuthbert. Like, for getting out of most of the exercises she assigns."

Cornwall looked startled. Nope, he must not have friends, not real ones, or he'd be used to ribbing.

"*C'mon,*" I said.

Slowly Cornwall broke into a grin, and we chuckled evilly together.

I had a feeling this was the start of a beautiful friendship.

I handed Cornwall back the now melted and sopping bag of peas. "Now that you and I are buddies, we're going to have a great old time," I said confidently. "The first thing we'll do is investigate the swamp. I've been dying to, but Angela's squeamish."

"But...the *swamp*? My clothes," Cornwall objected. "Mom will kill me."

I put my uninjured arm around his shoulders. "Cornwall, m'boy, you gotta relax. Forget about being so tidy. Lose that hair oil, for starters. You're too young to be a lounge lizard."

"Really?" His face brightened. "I hate the stuff, Dinah. It drips down the back of my neck. But Mother says that if I'm to get Vegas gigs, I have to look sophisticated."

No wonder Cornwall had swaggered so idiotically in front of Madge. He was trying to act sophisticated. At age thirteen? These stage mothers, I thought in disgust.

It occurred to me that both Cornwall's and Angela's maternal units fit the clichéd, but all too true, role of the pushy mom who pressures her kid to work, work, work at showbiz for the big break. Sure, the big break happens to the kid—as in big break*down*. I silently thanked my own dreamily bookish mother, to whom a regular kidhood for me was way more important than any kind of glittery success.

I scrabbled a hand through Cornwall's sticking-up, anemone-like hair. "This is the look you want," I advised. "Messy and I-don't-care. The girls'll love it."

"Maybe 'When I'm sixty-four,'" sang Cornwall, from the lyrics of a Beatles song, and grinned.

"Nice pipes you got there," I complimented him. "You'd be one wicked lounge singer, Corny."

"Thanks, Dinah." He looked embarrassed. "Uh, I'd like to explain something. I know it seems weird, the way I read aloud from that book on Roger Bannister. But, see, Roger's kind of my idol. In school, in 1940s England, he was this pasty, flabby, loser-like kid, like me. Everybody laughed at him. But the whole time he was dreaming of breaking the record for running a mile. He practiced and practiced running because he believed in himself. That inspirational stuff you hear me reading—it's advice Roger gave other unconfident people after he succeeded."

"He broke the record?" I said disbelievingly. Somehow this Bannister guy, flabby, pasty, didn't sound like the Speedy Gonzalez type.

Cornwall beamed. "He didn't break it, Dinah. He shattered it, on May 6, 1954, at Oxford. Roger—later *Sir* Roger—became the first person in history to run a mile in under four minutes. What a hero, all the more since he was such an *unlikely* hero. Hey, and just a few years ago, in his seventies, he carried the Olympic torch through London."

I was about to utter an exclamation, but from far away the Howler did it for me. "AAAA-OOOOOO!"

Behind us, the whishing sound of sliding doors opening onto the deck. Mrs. Cuthbert appeared, blinking dazedly in the moonlight. "I *thought* I heard yelling," she said grumpily. "And now the Howler's chimed in. Noise everywhere! Dinah, Cornwall, what's going on?"

"Uh," I said, "we were re-enacting Phil Spector's Wall of Sound?"

Cornwall blurted, "What happened was that— YEOW!"

I'd given him a pinch in the arm. I didn't want him blurting a play-by-play of the night's events. If he did, he'd be confirming Beak-Nose's presence on the island, which Mrs. Cuthbert, up to now, thought I'd invented. Mrs. Cuthbert would have no choice but to send all of us home, for our safety, not to mention her sanity.

And I didn't want to leave. Not when I'd got closer to nabbing Beak-Nose. Not when I knew I had a mysterious ally somewhere on the island.

Another howl ripped the air. And not, I thought, my skin tingling with excitement, when there was the Howler to investigate.

Using my uninjured arm, I scooped up the baseball and began tossing and catching it. "We were perfecting our pitching skills," I lied glibly.

The fitness instructor clutched her head. "Obviously Angela and I are the only ones around here who sleep." Mrs. Cuthbert trudged off, shaking her head. "You two are playing catch…Dot Bridey's taking a marathon shower…"

Stunned, I hissed to Cornwall, "Did you hear that? Why would Dot Bridey be showering? *Unless she had something to scrub off her skin and hair in a mega-hurry.*"

I mulled this over the next morning. Could *Dot* Bridey be the stalker? I wondered, stirring the spoon around in my cottage cheese and fruit. Maybe she was stalking me on her sister-in-law's behalf. But why would she do such a thing—wasn't that taking family favors a bit too far?

I narrowed my eyes at Dot across Mrs. Cuthbert's picnic table, where all of us, except Angela, were breakfasting. Dot's hands, now ripping apart a croissant, were red and raw.

I held up the butter dish and said, "Care for some oil paint? Oh, silly me. I mean *butter*."

Dot's brown eyes, so like Angela's, fixed on me. Only, *un*like Angela's, they were bullet-hard and menacing…

She knows that I know, I thought. But…if Dot's the stalker, where's Beak-Nose? Why bother with an "ultimate disguise" if you have someone carrying out your revenge for you?

Then it came to me. Beak-Nose had gloated, *I've concocted the ultimate disguise for revenge.* The ultimate disguise was…somebody else! No wonder Beak-Nose had been so confident I wouldn't clue in. She'd delegated her revenge to her sister-in-law.

I remembered what Angela had said about not being able to go for auditions in the months following Vi's arrest. *The Bridey name was too notorious. And Mommy, who's always pushing me to succeed, was ballistic.*

I stared at Dot Bridey till she flinched. Dot viciously ripped the croissant into about a dozen more pieces. Then she left the table without eating any of them.

"Poor Dot," sympathized Mrs. Cuthbert. "So very worried about Angela."

More like, so very *vengeful*, I thought. I bet Beak-Nose wasn't here on Salt Spring at all. The police were right.

That explained, too, why no one had seen a beak-nosed woman hurrying out of the SkyTrain station.

It was an *un*beak-nosed woman, Dot, who had shoved me toward the tracks! Dot had left the auditions early to shop, she'd told Angela.

Shop, schmop, I thought indignantly. I was not only figuring out this mystery, I was Dotting the i's on it.

As Dot opened the sliding doors to go inside, snores from Angela's bedroom roared out to the deck. Cornwall observed, "At least we know Angela's catching up on her sleep—if not slaughtering it."

Our gazes met. He raised his hands and pretended to fend off the snores. Disloyally to Angela, I wanted badly to laugh. The memory of *Snore like a boar, Boardey!* stopped me. Just.

"Odd," Mrs. Cuthbert said suddenly. "Someone's placed my potted mums on top of the hot tub."

The mums, formerly at the front of the house, were conveniently hiding the yellow hand imprint on the hot-tub cover. When Mrs. Cuthbert wasn't around, I'd scrub the imprint off with paint thinner. "I did that," I said quickly. "Flowers on hot tubs. It's a principle of feng shui. A new one," I added, as Mrs. Cuthbert proceeded to frown doubtfully.

"We-ell, I guess we can leave them there for a while. But really, Dinah, I've studied feng shui myself and never heard of a *plant* being an active force—"

At that moment a bunch of leaves bobbed round the side of the house and shouted, "Yo! Hi, Di!"

Pantelli removed his baseball cap, which was thickly pasted over with leaves. "It's part of my new, plant-friendly dendrologist's gear," Pantelli explained, placing the cap on the picnic table.

He also had the large green nylon backpack he never went anywhere without. He kept his tree books and notes inside, as well as his digital camera, with a special zoom lens for capturing close-ups of bark and leaves.

He grimaced at my bowl of cottage cheese and fruit. "Like, *yech*, Dinah." He reached for a croissant. "You've heard of talking to plants? Prince Charles does. I figure, why not go Prince Chuck a step further? *Look* like 'em. They'll be more comfortable with you."

"This is my friend Pantelli," I said rather weakly and introduced him to Cornwall and Mrs. Cuthbert. "Er, Pantelli—why aren't you at science camp?"

Pantelli slathered blueberry jam on the croissant. "They're covering stuff I already know." He shrugged. "So I thought I'd sneak off and visit you. Well, not *just* you," he corrected himself. A soft, silly expression came over his face. "Also Angela. Have you noticed that her skin is the same shade as birch bark?"

From his backpack, Pantelli produced a round object messily wrapped and masking-taped in the *Vancouver Sun* weekend color comics. "This is for Angela," he announced. "Can I see her?"

With a last glance at his leaf-cap, Mrs. Cuthbert made a strange choking sound, almost sob-like, and gathered up the paper plates and plastic cups she was now having us use. She'd explained that she might as well try to preserve what was left of her china.

"Whoa," Pantelli commented admiringly after Cornwall and I filled him in on Beak-Nose's activities to date. "Hurling rocks at you, Di. And menacing you at midnight. I *told* Talbot you'd be having all the fun."

The three of us approached Angela's room. Her door was open: she was sitting up in bed, smiling wanly at her mom.

"So what's the gift?" I murmured to Pantelli. "It's not anything that crawls, is it? Angela's not what you're used to. She's dainty."

"It's the newest, state-of-the-art Zap-O-Fume-O stink cushion," Pantelli whispered back, out of the side of his mouth.

"What? Angela won't like that." I grabbed it from him and held it behind my back.

Dot Bridey was fidgeting with pillows to make Angela more comfortable. "You should be putting songs on your tapes," she was fretting.

These stage mothers! "Aw, give the kid a rest," I protested.

Dot whipped her gaze around to me. She started to retort, but Angela said, smiling, "Hey, Pantelli. Great to see you!" She squinted at his leafy headgear. "Nice, um…"

"Plant-friendly cap," Pantelli explained. He then proceeded to blather on about his new approach to tree care. Angela was too polite to interrupt him.

Cornwall gave a rude snort, muttered something about catching up on his reading and strode off.

Which left me hanging back in the hallway on my own, musing. A marathon shower would've got the paint off Dot's face and hands.

But not off her cloak. Not that permanent oil paint.

Dot, sitting next to Angela on the bed with a pained smile, was absorbing Pantelli's lengthy lecture on trees. "Prince Charles recommended talking to plants way back in the eighties," my buddy was saying. Pantelli waved his cap for emphasis, not noticing that leaves were becoming unstuck and flying off. "I've e'd Chuck that it's time to go beyond mere talk. We have to *empathize*."

I slipped quietly down the hall to Dot Bridey's room and shut the door behind me.

Chapter Thirteen

Cloaked in Suspicion

Realizing I still held Pantelli's ridiculous gift, I placed it on the bed carefully, so as not to break the plastic casing. The new, improved Dinah would never explode one of these bombs, which smell like—well, let's just say like the aftereffects of too many baked beans. Along with Pantelli and Talbot, the old, unimproved Dinah had booby-trapped several foes with Zap-O-Fume-Os. For instance, we'd put one under the patio-chair cushion of snippy Liesl Dubuque, who lived next door to me in East Van.

Liesl's shrieks still echoed satisfyingly in my mind...

But I shoved such immature thoughts aside. I was determined to be dignified and responsible, like Angela. Zap-O-Fume-Os were out from now on.

I lifted the neatly folded clothes in Dot's chest of drawers. Shorts, Ts, underwear. A box of audition tapes, some labeled—*Angela Bridey sings Tosca, Angela Bridey sings La Bohème*, etcetera—and some blank.

Something rattled when I replaced the box. In the far corner of the drawer, I saw a bottle of prescription pills. *Anti-depressants*, the label read.

No cloak, though.

I shut the drawers and checked Dot's suitcase. Bathing suit, beach towels. A gold appointment book. Flipping through it, I saw a lot of appointments, all right—with a Dr. MacGillicuddy in the University of British Columbia Hospital's psychiatric ward.

I whistled. Well, at least Dot *knew* she had mental problems. Still, no cloak in sight, not yet.

Replacing the appointment book, I checked the stacks of extra towels and sheets on the closet shelf. Nothing.

Then...footsteps in the hall. Growing louder. Reaching the bedroom door.

On the other side of the door, Dot said sharply, "I heard a whistle. *Someone's in my room.*"

The doorknob began to turn.

I dove under the bed, remembering just in time to take Pantelli's Zap-O-Fume-O with me.

Two pairs of feet appeared at the end of the bed. "I can't have people intruding in my room," Dot Bridey snapped. "That's a condition of Angela's and my remaining here, Ethel. I hope you made that clear to Dinah and Cornwall."

"I didn't have to," Mrs. Cuthbert replied. Impatiently she began tapping one flip-flopped foot on the carpet. "Both Dinah and Cornwall are good kids at heart."

Boy, did I feel guilty. I'd betrayed the fitness instructor's good opinion of me, and for nothing. There was no paint-stained cloak in the room.

Dot Bridey's running-shoed feet marched to her suitcase; with a slight cracking of knee joints, she bent to survey the contents. I saw her long fingers scrabbling through the side compartments. Had I put the appointment book back in the right compartment?

Dropping the suitcase lid shut, Dot stood again. "Maybe what I heard was a bird," she remarked grudgingly.

Phew. That'd been way too close for comfort. I used the cloth that happened to be beside me to mop sweat from my forehead.

Whoa. That was no cloth. *It was the Night Stalker's cloak.* Even amid the shadowy dust balls, the paint I'd streaked all over it glowed luridly.

But in pulling the cloak toward me, I'd disturbed a dust ball. I watched, helpless, as it cartwheeled out from under the bed...

"WHERE DID THAT COME FROM?" Dot demanded.

"Sorry if I don't vacuum according to your standards," Mrs. Cuthbert retorted. I could tell she'd had enough of Dot.

"*Someone's under the bed, you idiot,*" Dot snapped. "I *knew* I heard a whistle."

And in front of me, both sets of legs began to bend.

I froze. I was clutching the cloak with one hand, while with the other I still held Pantelli's Zap-O-Fume-O.

The Zap-O-Fume-O.

Dot's knees creaked as they descended. One more second and I'd be detected.

A preemptive strike was the only option. I smashed down on the Zap-O-Fume-O with both hands. Plastic casing and wrapping paper tore; the Zap-O's patented deadly clear gas gushed forth.

"GOOD LORD, WOMAN," choked Mrs. Cuthbert, staggering away.

Dot Bridey stumbled out of the room after her. "Nice try, Ethel," she coughed. "That lollapalooza was yours. Try some Gas-X in the future, why don't you."

They collapsed into the hall and, with an agonized gasp about calling fumigators, Mrs. Cuthbert slammed the door.

I scrambled out Dot's window. I'd been holding my breath all this time: another benefit of those endless singing exercises. Landing on the deck, I expelled the breath noisily.

Pantelli zoomed round from the carport. "So you activated the Zap-O-Fume-O," he said in admiration. "Awesome. Not for nothing is it called the 'deluxe edition.'"

He was waving a *Girl Athletes' Annual* to waft away the Zap-O-Fume-O fumes. I said crossly, "Don't tell me you're into reading that."

"Huh? Naw, I was reading it aloud to Angela. She asked me to," Pantelli said, pleased. "She said my voice would soothe her to sleep. Though," he added reflectively, "in my last glimpse of Angela, she, her mom and Mrs. Cuthbert were fleeing up the driveway."

Pantelli and I sat down on the deck stairs. He glanced at the blackberry bushes. "Wonder if the Zap-O-Fume-O will shrivel the fruit," he mused in the thoughtful tone he adopted when feeling scientific.

"Wonder if I'll ever be dignified like Angela," I mourned. "I was trying so hard, Pantelli. But there was the Zap-O-Fume-O, and what was I to do?"

"Angela. Yeah." Pantelli beamed. "She's serious, quiet, polite…not at all like you, Di. More like Shandi, I'd say. I think Shandi's seriousness is what attracted Talbot to her—that, and her being an intellectual. Like, I overheard Shandi telling Tal all about the arguments for irrigation versus leaving natural wetlands alone."

"Great," I said bitterly. "With Alberta Einstein in his life, Talbot won't be bothered ever thinking about me again." I supposed these feelings of jealousy were a sign that womanly emotions were dawning in me.

I always knew that womanhood was going to be a bore.

With difficulty I shelved the jealousy and instead told Pantelli about finding the telltale cloak in Dot Bridey's room.

"Wow," he said. "Dot Bridey subbing for Beak-Nose. That's the ultimate disguise, all right. Hey, you gotta talk to the police, Dinah."

"Yeah, except Dot's on to me. She'd stash or destroy the cloak before Constable Leary ever got here. I need more proof," I sighed.

There was a moment's silence between us. Through the open trailer door, we heard Cornwall reading aloud.

"'The reason sport is attractive to many of the general public is that it's filled with reversals. What you think may happen doesn't happen. A champion is beaten, an unknown becomes a champion.

"'A champion is beaten,'" Cornwall repeated. "'An unknown becomes a champion.'"

"O-kaaaaay," said Pantelli. Leaning toward the trailer, he opened his mouth to shout something rude.

"Sssshhh," I said. "Cornwall's reading quotations from Roger Bannister for inspiration."

Pantelli gave me a strange look. I didn't blame him. I realized I'd actually sounded tolerant about someone. A first for me. Maybe this growing-up business wasn't so bad. In tiny amounts, mind you.

We rounded up Cornwall and, at Pantelli's suggestion, rowed around the south end of St. Mary Lake. It took about a microsecond for Pantelli to obsess on the swamp. "Cool! Get a load of the healthy reed stalks," he breathed. "And hey, did you guys know cypress trees are able to grow in swamps?" Raising his binoculars, he squinted eagerly through, as if checking for saplings.

"Did you know that idiots are able to grow in rowboats?" Cornwall shot back, clearly bored.

Sediment scraped the bottom of the boat. "Um, Pantelli," I said. If we got stuck, I really didn't feel like squelching out of the swamp in my standard Cuthbert's Fitness Retreat footgear—that is to say, bare feet.

"It's fine, Di." Propping the oars on his seat, Pantelli lay back, using his backpack for a pillow. "Go on, Corny. Entertain us. What was it you were reciting? 'A moron should never give up. With a little effort, a moron can become a champion loser.'"

Cornwall turned tomato red and began shouting insults at Pantelli. I gritted my teeth and considered what the new, improved, Angela-like Dinah would do. Probably reason with both boys in a soft, persuasive, sweetly patient voice.

Stuff that.

"BE QUIET OR I'LL SHOVE YOU GUYS OVERBOARD!" I yelled.

In response, from somewhere on the ranch property—a long howl.

Pantelli jumped, gazing round in astonishment. "What is this, the set of *The Hound of the Baskervilles*?" he asked. His backpack, no longer weighted to the stern by his elbow, toppled overboard.

Chapter Fourteen

The (Mis)fortune-teller

Pantelli shrugged off losing his backpack. "It happens," he said, pushing away from the swamp with a vigorous backswing of oars.

My buddy-since-toddlerhood looked uncomfortable, though. He was being like Talbot, suffering misfortune in honorable silence so as not to bother anyone. If it were me, I'd be yelling in frustration. I felt really sorry for Pantelli. "We could pull the backpack out," I suggested. "Dry your books off in the sun."

Pantelli managed a wan grin. "Hang up *Trees of the Pacific Northwest*, Fifth Edition, with clothes-pegs? Nah." He brightened. "Hey, that gives me an idea for an invention. Waterproof books. Naturalists would love that. So would clumsy boaters. I'd make millions."

"You're trying to change the subject, Pantelli. Which means you're being noble," I said sternly. "It doesn't suit you."

"Rough break, Pantelli," Cornwall said. "Er, sorry I insulted you, y'know, about your trees 'n' stuff."

"That's okay," Pantelli told him. "Sorry I made fun of your self-esteem 'n' stuff."

"Puh-leeze," I begged them. "Any more of this and we'll all be crying and hugging like on *Dr. Phil.*"

Before Pantelli left, I made him borrow the Galloway family digital camera. "Till you get another camera of your own," I insisted, thinking of Pantelli's mud- and water-clogged one sitting at the bottom of St. Mary Lake. "There must be some, I dunno, irregularly patterned bark you'll want to photograph at science camp."

I saw he was reluctant to take my camera, so I threatened to clobber him if he didn't. Worked like a charm (taking notes, Dr. Phil?). Pantelli trotted off with the camera in his back pocket, waving to me and Cornwall and gazing with adoration at Angela's pale face in her bedroom window. She'd staggered over to see him off.

Angela was thawing toward Pantelli, I reflected. I mean, who *couldn't* like a tree nut? Now that Pantelli had left, I suddenly felt lonely and missed him a lot. Ditto Talbot, even if he was—I fingered my pop-can-ring necklace—devoting himself to this Shandi person 24/7.

Then I did what any lonely person does in the twenty-first century. I decided to check my e-mail. It'd mean a bicycle trip into Ganges, to the Salt Spring Roasting Company Café—in other words, hearty exercise. But hey, I was desperate.

Also, I could make inquiries about Madame Sosostris. There was something fishy about that incident at her stall. Maybe *she* was the one who'd slipped me the note.

Cornwall, buried in his trailer, didn't want to come with me. He was alternating between reading aloud—

"'The man who can drive himself further once the effort gets painful is the man who will win'"—and crooning the Olympics promotional song Mrs. Beechum had sent us to practice. I hadn't got around to it yet.

Snores charged like rampaging cattle from Angela's room. I guessed that fleeing up the driveway, then staggering to the window to wave good-bye to Pantelli, had been too much for her. I lied briskly to Mrs. Cuthbert about merely taking a spin to the end of Tripp Road—and set off in the other direction.

At a public phone booth, I leafed through the Gulf Islands Yellow Pages for Madame Sosostris. Bingo. Her number: 250-FOR-TUNE. I tried it and got a cackling message asking me to leave my phone and credit card numbers. "Madame Sosostris will consult your personal stars and get back to you with a reading," Velma finished.

Call me a skeptic, but as far as I was concerned, my personal stars could stick to twinkling. I headed for Velma's house, at the top of yet another hill, on a winding street several blocks past Centennial Park.

At Velma's purple-painted door, I felt it again. That sense of being watched.

I swung around to peer at the garden. Rows of purple pansies stretched from the tall surrounding hedge to the path. The air was still and hot.

For just a moment, part of the hedge at the side of the house rustled...

"YOU!" Velma shrieked, glaring at me from the now open door.

I would have jumped except that, after all that biking, my muscles were in shutdown. "Er, yeah," I said, dragging my glance away from the hedge. I plastered on a fake friendly smile. "Sorry about the hair wrenching the other day. I thought you were someone I knew."

"I see. That's something you do to your *friends*." Velma held up a hand weighted with purple plastic rings before I could respond. "Never mind. We'll let bygones be bygones. Come on in; I've been expecting you."

"Wow," I commented, impressed, "you really are psychic!"

"I try," Velma said modestly and waved me into a living room darkened with star-studded, hanging, purple sheets. Noticing my stare, she explained, "Purple channels the spirits."

She sat me down and plunked a heavy crystal ball into my hands.

I raised my eyebrows. "So...the spirits want to play catch?"

"*No*," Velma returned frostily. "Step one is for you to transmit yourself to the spirit world. Now relax... concentrate on what it is you want..." Still standing, she shut her eyes and began humming and swaying.

What I wanted, very badly, was something to drink. Oh, and maybe a snack.

"...concentrate on what you want..."

But concentrating was only making me thirstier and hungrier. On the other hand, I didn't want to interrupt Velma's trance. I'd heard you weren't supposed to interrupt a sleepwalker; they suffered a terrible shock if you did. Maybe it was the same with trancing psychics.

I carefully set the crystal ball beside me on Velma's purple sofa. Then, quietly getting up, I tiptoed into her kitchen. Even a piece of bread would be great. Velma wouldn't mind, would she? After all, she'd been expecting me, and you always offer guests food.

The kitchen wasn't swathed in lurid purples. It was a nice cheery yellow. Over the sink, a big window was flung open, letting in the mingled scent of pansies and cedar hedge.

And—eureka! On the windowsill, a blackberry pie sat cooling. By the sink were two plates, two napkins, two forks, two cups. A teapot, with a purple knitted tea cozy over it, sent up slow curls of steam.

Well! It was obvious Velma meant to feed me. She wouldn't mind if I had a weeny pie slice right now, would she? Besides, I concentrated better, on the spirits or anything else for that matter, when not hungry.

I was just tucking into a hearty wedge of pie when the doorbell rang. Patting my mouth with a napkin, I started for the door. No reason for Velma to stop her humming and swaying.

But Velma got there first. I watched from the kitchen as a teenage girl stepped inside. "I'm ready to find out whether Herbert really loves me," she announced between loud cracks of gum.

In the meantime, behind me, there was a strange *whish* and a thud. I didn't have time to look around, because Velma spun, spotted me in the kitchen doorway and frowned.

She turned back to the girl. "You mean *you* booked the appointment at two? *You're* Suzy?"

"Yeah. Sorry I'm late, Madame Sosostris. My visit to the orthodontist took longer than I expected." The girl pulled back her lips, revealing upper and lower teeth covered with silver.

"Then who is—"

But I didn't stay to hear the rest of Velma's sentence or the explosion of her temper that no doubt followed. There was a door out the side of the kitchen, and I zoomed for it.

Not before noticing, though, that the rest of the blackberry pie had vanished off the windowsill…

Chapter Fifteen

Too Many Right Moves

"The weird thing was, as I bicycled away—at rip-roaring speed, natch—a piercing howl filled the neighborhood."

I was relating my escape to a wide-eyed Angela and Cornwall. Angela was sitting upright in her bed. A checkerboard lay on the comforter. Angela had just finished a triple jump of Cornwall's pieces. "The Howler," Angela breathed, frightened. "Where did the howl come from?"

A *Girl Athletes' Annual* was about to slide off the comforter. I retrieved it and began flipping through its pages, with nervous energy rather than any desire to read. "The howl seemed to come from Velma's house," I said, scrunching my glasses farther up my nose in an effort to remember.

With Velma chasing after me, her long purple skirt crackling about her legs and her wild tresses flying, I'd been too scared to pay much attention to the howl's source. *Give me back my pie!* Velma had shrieked.

I'd never bicycled so fast. If I were interested in being an Olympics participant, bicycling would be my sport. I must've surpassed Lance Armstrong's personal best by a long shot.

Okay, so I'd been going downhill. Effort counts for something.

"And I only had a piece of the pie, not the whole thing," I muttered. "So that's another mystery: what was that *whish* at the windowsill, and where did the rest of the pie go?"

Really, I thought, it was as puzzling as Pantelli's nonchalance about dropping his backpack in the lake.

"If you're going to talk about pie, I'm leaving," Cornwall said, annoyed. He packed up the checkers game and headed outside to his trailer.

Sighing, I glanced down at *Girl Athletes' Annual*. I'd absently flipped to a story called "Elsie the Hiker Gets Lost." In the illustrations, Elsie was a mini-skirted tween with a puffed-up hairdo and neon pink fishnet stockings. Like, really practical gear for hiking. I scanned the story. For marking forest trails, Elsie used hair ribbons. A real tomboy, all right.

I shut the book with an impatient snap that echoed through the house.

It occurred to me how very quiet the house was.

"Hey, where's your mom? Where's Mrs. Cuthbert?" I demanded.

Angela lowered her gaze and plucked uneasily at the comforter. "They went to look for you, Dinah. They realized you'd been gone an awfully long time for just cycling along the lake."

"Uh-oh," I said weakly. I'd broken the cardinal Cuthbert rule: no leaving the neighborhood. I might as well pack up my *Joey the Homicidal Android* graphic novels and other belongings right now.

A feeling of defeat came over me, more painful than my sore muscles. I hadn't proved Dot Bridey was the stalker. And I didn't have the heart to question Angela: *Thanks for taking that bash on the head for me, and by the way, is your mom a vengeful psycho?* Even the old, unimproved Dinah wouldn't be that tactless.

"It's been great knowing you, Angela," I said. "I tried so hard to be like you, but…" I shrugged. "I better go stuff my things in my suitcase."

Then I brightened, sort of. "That's the advantage of leaving most of your stuff packed. It gets wrinkled, sure, but you can leave in a flash."

Exit on a wisecrack, that's me.

Piling my *Joey the Homicidal Android* graphic novels in my suitcase, I realized I'd failed on another front too. I hadn't lived up to my Olympic challenge of dieting, what with the weeny—okay, not so weeny—piece of blackberry pie I'd helped myself to at Velma's.

Though blackberry pie couldn't be all that bad, I rationalized, rolling up my *Judy at Carnegie Hall* poster. Or raspberry squares or apple crumble, say. Or figgy pudding.

Figs. Now where had I heard figs mentioned recently?

In Talbot's e-mail.

A slight change in what's around you can mean a lot. Take Emperor Augustus Caesar, who noticed his fig tree was gleaming brighter than usual in the sun—only he didn't pay attention. And look what happened. I told you about him, right?

Right, I thought. And now I remembered about Augustus Caesar not clueing in to the newly gleaming figs. Fail, Caesar. He should have. His wife, the Empress Livia, had painted poison on them. Augustus tucked into the figs, and…kaput.

*A slight change in what's around you…*I gripped the suitcase zipper. There'd been a slight change around here today. Just now in Angela's room. *She'd triple-jumped Cornwall.* Angela, who was hopeless at checkers.

The phone screeched. Angela, who'd got up to mix some iced tea in the kitchen, answered it.

"DINAH!" She appeared at the door, her solemn eyes bulging with alarm. She thrust the phone into my hands. "It's—it's Pantelli. *He's in trouble.*"

Not being in the best of moods, my first thought was unkind. Pantelli had misplaced a leaf specimen, say. As Angela hurried out, I grabbed the phone. "Listen, Pantelli, I want to get outta here before Mrs. Cuthbert returns. I—"

"Dinah. You gotta come help me. I'm in trouble. A big branch fell on top of me and I can't move. I think my ankle's broken. Dinah…"

There was a crashing sound, as if he had dropped the phone. "But where are you?" I shouted.

Angela reappeared at the door. She'd pulled shorts on and was tucking her nightgown into the waist. "Pantelli's across the lake, at that deserted ranch. The poor guy stammered that out at the beginning of the call." She held up some rolled-up beach towels. "We can wrap his leg in these; it'll be less painful for him."

We hurried out toward the dock, which seemed achingly far away now that there was an emergency.

"Whuzzup?" Cornwall called from a trailer window. He was holding his Roger Bannister book.

"Help us," I yelled.

Slipping away from the window, he pushed at the slightly ajar trailer door and—*wham*. Another can of maple syrup, open at the top, fell on him.

Cornwall lifted his arms, hunching his sopping head between his shoulders. "Very funny," he fumed. "So much for us being friends, Dinah Galloway!"

I swiveled to protest, "It wasn't me," and knew he wouldn't believe me.

Angela and I ran, though not as fast as I would have liked. Angela was holding on to the bandaged part of her head and swaying. I thought of telling her to go back to the house; this was too much for her. Then I thought, When we find Pantelli, one of us can stay with him while the other goes for help. So I didn't say anything.

Instead, in frustration, I twisted the pop-can ring on my cord necklace as we semi-ran. "What was Pantelli doing across the lake?" I demanded. "I thought he was going back to his science camp on Mayne."

"Collecting specimens, maybe?"

It was Angela, not nervous, butterfingers me, who gracefully untied the rowboat's mooring from the rusted steel hook at dock's edge. Angela was the cool-headed, efficient one, I reflected in admiration. I rowed us across, clumsy in my panic.

Partway across the lake, I realized that my jittery flailing at the oars, each stroke totally out of synch with the other, wasn't moving us very fast. The rowboat was wrenching left and right as much as progressing. I heaved a deep breath to calm myself and tried again.

"You're white-knuckling the oars, Dinah," Angela said sympathetically. "Your poor hands are going to be blistered. When we get back, I'll lend you one of my hand creams."

"Great," I said. I didn't want to be rude, but I was really more interested in finding Pantelli than swathing my paws in Estée Lauder.

I yanked at the oars...Had to reach the ranch...

The sun was baking my forehead; sweat ran into my eyes. As Angela brushed water flecks off her shorts, I squeezed my eyes shut, the better to concentrate on rowing.

The way any last image does when you close your peepers, the one of Angela brushing water off stayed with me. She sure had nice hands.

I thought of all the hands that had waved at me lately, some in a friendly way, some not. There were Mrs. Beechum's stubby hands, parting the auditioners like the Red Sea. There were Beak-Nose's large-knuckled hands, reaching through the bulrushes. There were Cornwall's hands, hanging limply both times he'd been doused with a falling can of maple syrup. Velma's bony hands; Dot Bridey's long, nervous ones.

Pantelli's hands, splaying at me in mockery of Beak-Nose's threat: *the talons of vengeance will sink into you...*

Of course, Pantelli didn't have talons. He was a nail-biter like me. Like Cornwall.

I thought of Dot Bridey's red, raw, nervous hands. Her nails were blunt.

Eyes still scrunched shut, I pictured Beak-Nose stretching her bony hands through the ferns at Trout Lake.

Her nails, too, were blunt...

I opened my eyes. Unaware that I was looking at her, Angela had spread both her own pretty hands out and was studying them with pleasure. Studying the smooth skin and the lovely, polished, U-shaped nails.

I stared at them. They were great long ones, like boardwalks. Angela had...

Talons.

The rowboat's bow crashed against the dock.

"Oopsie!" Angela cooed, giggling. "Overshot yourself, huh, Dinah?"

"I was busy thinking about checkers, among other things," I said, resting the oars on my knees. I was panting, so she might or might not have been able to hear the tension in my voice. I didn't really care.

"Checkers?" Angela was deftly tying the rope to a leg of the dock.

"Yeah. Nice triple jump in your game with Cornwall."

Angela giggled. She climbed up the ladder to the dock and stood, smiling down at me. Waiting, the way *It* does in hide-and-seek when she knows she's got you.

I sat in the rowboat for a moment longer. "Your mother," I said. "She isn't the one who tried pushing me in front of SkyTrain. She isn't the Night Stalker. It's you. *You're Violet Bridey's avenger.*"

Angela stepped into the shade at the edge of the woods. "I was broken up about the scandal, Dinah. I told you, 'member? How other kids made fun of me, calling me Devilla because I had a criminal in the family? Being a Bridey, I couldn't go to auditions for the longest time."

She stepped back farther into the shadows. I had to climb up to the dock to see her.

Angela said, "How stupid you've been. Yes, it was me all along. I even slipped you that creepy note at the Witherspoon Agency—you thought it was someone in a carrot costume. That 'carrot' was a vegan auditioner, you idiot!

"Mommy's been so worried about me. Knowing how close I am to Aunt Vi, she suspects I'm obsessed with revenge. That's why Mommy keeps urging me to concentrate on my career. *She wants me to forget about what you did to Aunt Vi.*"

Angela erupted in a prolonged giggle—one that rose to a high pitch and cracked into hee-hees. "When Mommy brought me to Salt Spring, I begged her to detour to Mount Maxwell Provincial Park. We'd been there before, and I had a beautiful ink-dark idea, as Auntie would say, about how to remove myself from your suspicions.

"I ran way ahead of Mommy, to this meadow I'd read about in a guidebook. I headed for a Garry oak at the meadow's edge. I'd brought a rope. I tied one end round and round a rock and then tossed the other end over a branch. I hauled the rock up till it sat nicely on the branch; I pushed the loose end of rope around the back of the trunk, out of sight.

"Later, when you and I were at the park, I pretended to see someone behind us. I tugged on the rope—and pushed you out of the way. I made you believe I'd rescued you and had been hit in the process. From then on, there was no way you wouldn't trust me."

Across the lake, Cornwall was splashing about by Mrs. Cuthbert's dock. Washing the maple syrup off, I guessed. He was sure getting practiced in that by now.

I stood up in the boat, bracing my feet on either side to keep the rocking down. "CORNWALL!" I yelled.

The opposite side was far, but my voice could go farther. "CORNWALL! SEND HELP!"

He stared. He yelled something back. I couldn't hear what, but I figured it wasn't warm and fuzzy.

"You're wasting your time," Angela said sharply. "Cornwall's mad at you for dumping more maple syrup on him. He's not going to help." She preened. "I positioned that can, just like I did the first one, to pit Mrs. Cuthbert and Cornwall against you.

"When you disappear, I'll say you ran off. We'll all tell the police how wild you were. How uncontrollable. The type who was a natural target for trouble."

Beak-Nose had also used the word "target." *Sweet, vicious revenge, with you as the target.*

Coincidence? But I didn't have time to think about that right now.

"PLEASE," I yelled. Cornwall was climbing back onto Mrs. Cuthbert's dock. I tried to think of how to appeal to him in two seconds or less, using limited-syllable, megawatt volume.

Cornwall was walking away, shaking water off his head and his arms. He'd retreat to his trailer, towel off and take comfort in reading aloud from his Roger Bannister book.

Roger Bannister, the runner who believed in his own personal best when no one else did.

I heaved the biggest breath I'd ever taken and belted out: "BELIEVE THE BEST OF ME, CORNWALL. PLEASE!"

He didn't turn.

"It's no use," Angela said.

She was deeper into the woods by now. Her smile was—well, angelic, as always. But her dark eyes, usually wide, were narrowed and cunning, like those of an old woman. A bitter, watching one.

The water, sparkling with sun, lapped at the rowboat. I *could* row back and get help myself. It was so tempting to put distance between myself and that sly girl, that *It*, waiting in the shade.

But Pantelli was in trouble. And I had a very strong feeling that Angela had something to do with it.

I walked over to join her, and the ink-dark shadows of the firs covered us.

Chapter Sixteen

The Howler, Revealed

To the right of the forest stretched pasture. We walked in the opposite direction, the woods closing more and more thickly around us. "Pantelli said he was up this way," Angela prattled happily. "Several hundred yards to the northwest."

I knew there was something wrong. Angela couldn't possibly care about Pantelli. Until his visit here, she'd made her dislike of him plain. Come to think of it, why *had* she turned nicey-nice today, asking him to read aloud to her?

But for now I wasn't concerned with Angela's mood changes. "Your Aunt Violet is nowhere near Salt Spring, is she? Pantelli joked about her being 'Super Beak,' able to outwit the police and sneak onto the island. But super-people exist only in comic books. Your Aunt Vi never intended to follow me."

"Of course not," Angela said. "*I* did. She and I arranged it. We both hate you, Dinah."

Yet Angela was making no menacing moves toward me. If anything, she was giving me an unusually wide berth as we tramped through the woods. Angela mused, "Aunt Vi's probably back east by now, in one of her disguises. An elderly waitress maybe. Or a piano teacher in the bloom of youth.

"I learned about disguises from Aunt Vi," she confided. "She coached me in acting too. But even with all that, and my Royal Opera Society-trained voice, you were the kid grabbing all the attention. You, the red-hot redhead. Always you."

"Um," I said, trying to ignore the past tense in *you were*. If I hadn't heard Pantelli say he was in trouble, I'd have serious doubts about following Angela—more like Devilla, as her classmates had called her—into this lonely forest.

"Pantelli," I called suddenly. "PANTELLI, WHERE ARE YOU?"

My voice echoed back to me. Angela smiled to herself. Her bandage kept slipping as she swayed. That crooked gait. Of course—the Night Stalker had lurched about too. Why hadn't it occurred to me that someone who couldn't walk in a straight line must be injured?

I thought of something else. "Your stalker appearances. We heard you snoring. So many other times too. It was like the heavy-metal take on sleep. Only…"

An encore of the hee-hees. "A tape recorder, silly! I taped the snoring off a CD of sound effects from the library. I pumped the volume way up and spun you that line about my snoring problem. You were so *sympathetic*, Dinah. 'Member?"

Oh, I 'membered, all right. I 'membered Dot's e-mail to Angela, praising her for her skill at recording and editing tapes.

"What about the kids on your school trip making fun of your snoring?" I demanded. "What about *Snore like a boar, Boardey*?"

Angela pursed her nostrils as if a bad smell were wafting beneath them. "*I* don't snore," she said, offended. "It was another girl who did. I taunted the girl about her problem, the twit cried and the teachers called Mommy to come and take me home. I didn't know how to get along with others, they said."

She stopped, gazing round. Noticing a mossy stump, she nodded at it and kept going. "Well, c'mon, Dinah! Don't want to rescue your tree-fanatic friend?"

Right. Angela was making fun of Pantelli—when *she* communicated with tree stumps. I was about to point this out, when I glanced at the stump myself.

A blue velvet hair ribbon was wedged between two jagged pieces of bark on the stump's rim. Just the kind of ribbon Angela twined through her long shiny tresses.

Angela had been here before. She'd marked a trail with hair ribbons, just like Elsie the Hiker.

Elsie. I gulped. Pantelli hadn't phoned for help. Angela had secretly recorded him reading "Elsie the Hiker Gets Lost" aloud to her. She could've easily recorded him saying my name, as well, and patched the two together.

She'd rung Mrs. Cuthbert's number from her cell. Then, grabbing the house phone, Angela had pretended that Pantelli was on the line, saying he was in trouble at the deserted property across the lake. She'd thrust the phone into my hands in time for me to hear him reading aloud from Elsie's adventures, the part where Elsie calls for help.

Pantelli hadn't dropped his phone in midsentence; Angela had clicked hers off.

"Well, come *on*," Angela urged. She was staring at me with those old-woman's eyes—and biting her lips to keep from grinning.

Quite the Devilla-ish sense of humor the girl had.

"I can't keep going just yet," I said suddenly.

I thought of my dream about Dad. Though I never quite viewed his appearances as dreams, exactly. More like guardian-angel-type visits. A flawed guardian angel, I grant you, given his fatal, alcohol-spurred car crash.

But a loving guardian angel nonetheless. And a savvy one. He'd said, *Your challenge will be to understand the stalker before she realizes you can.*

I couldn't let on to Angela that I was on to her Pantelli ruse.

I said to Angela, "I need a break." I heaved a few puffs to illustrate this point. In fact, all Mrs. Cuthbert's exercises had paid off. I was managing this hike without feeling winded.

Angela glared. "We don't have *time* for a break. And anyhow, we didn't bring any water. So let's just—"

"The way *I* take breaks is by bursting into song," I informed her. And then I belted out, "*London Bridge is falling down, falling down, falling down. London Bridge is falling down, my fair lady.*"

I proceeded into lots of refrains. Angela was goggling at me as if I were cracked. Well, there's good and bad cracked. I knew which category she belonged to.

"*London Bridge is—*"

From far down the slope, a howl. Or, as I'd thought of it in East Vancouver, where there weren't deep, echo-prone forests to turn it into a howl, an ascending-the-scale type of bark.

Brambles crunched. Another bark, some heavy, happy panting, and London bounded up to me.

I'd never been so glad to see anyone. I dove at London for a hug.

"What is this, an audition for *Lassie*?" Angela snapped. "*What's going on?*"

Not *Lassie*, I thought. Wrong story. That howl could only be a *Call of the Wild*, whose author, Jack London, the Butterwicks had quite logically named their pooch after.

But I saw no reason to launch into literary explanations. In any case, Angela was busy unrolling the beach towels she'd brought with her.

"It's just a stray dog," I fibbed. Straightening, I clapped my hands and ordered London, "GO!"

London tipped her head at me, puzzled. I sure wasn't being very playful, she was thinking.

"GO!" I commanded.

She went, crashing back over the brambles. I watched her silver coat flash between the evergreens till it dwindled to a speck and disappeared.

When I looked back, Angela had strung an arrow to a bow and was aiming it at me.

My throat, already in need of water, turned sand-dry. "Er...talk about your mood ruiners," I said.

"'The irrepressibly ebullient Dinah Galloway,'" Angela snapped. "Remember that review?"

"Remember it—I can't even *define* it." If I'd had any saliva left, I would have gulped. Angela appeared to be, shall we say, mildly obsessed with my supposedly successful career. "C'mon, I sing with dogs and I dodge pies."

"The reviewers love you. Always talented Dinah *this*, talented Dinah *that*," Angela complained—and let the arrow fly. I ducked but felt it *whoosh* past my right ear.

She strung another arrow. I galloped backward in probably the clumsiest attempt at an escape in history. Hmmm, I'd have to check with Talbot about that. *If* I got out of the forest before Robin Hood's evil female twin here zinged me. I was a target, just as Beak-Nose had promised.

"I thought you were a bad shot," I protested, stumbling round a tree. "Stupid me. You were a bad shot like you were a bad checkers player. All part of your disguise."

Whoosh! The next arrow Scud-missiled through the thick pine needles. The point missed me—just—but the feathers scraped my arm like a sting.

Gotta keep Angela talking, I decided, falling with a noisy "Oof!" over a craggy log. "So," I called chattily, picking myself up, "*you* were the Night Stalker."

"Yes. I wanted to freak you out, Dinah. Let you know that revenge, that *It*, was coming for you. But I didn't like being slathered with paint," she added crossly, zapping another arrow my way to punctuate her displeasure. *Boing!* This arrow plowed into the log and flapped wildly.

"An effective countermeasure, if a crude one," Angela continued. "It took me *ages* to shower the paint off. I got Mommy to cover for me, to say *she* was the one showering. She tried scrubbing the paint off my cloak—a gift from Aunt Vi—but only got her hands red and raw in the process.

"I told Mommy that if she didn't cover for me, I'd tell the Olympics promotional committee that I was seeing a psychiatrist for my obsessive tendencies. No way they'd give the opera-commercial gig to a kid of questionable mental stability. Hee hee!"

I could see Angela's yellow nightgown flashing through the pine needles. Yellow: not the shrewdest color to wear if you're stalking someone in a forest.

In a way, a tiny way, that made me feel better. Angela was smart, but not foolproof smart. Maybe I had a chance, if I could just do that un-Dinah thing and be stealthy.

"So your mom knew what you were doing?" I yelled and began creeping away from behind the tree.

Angela snorted. "I fooled her into thinking I didn't mean you any harm, that I was just having a few laughs sneaking around at night. She guessed that I unleashed that rock on my own head. Now she's terrified that I—get this—might be trying to harm *myself*! That's why she's sticking around. Hee hee hee!"

Somehow I couldn't bring myself to politely join in the yuks. I lobbed a stick as far as I could to the left. There was a thud as it hit the bottom of a trunk. A whirl of yellow in that direction. *Zinnggg!* An arrow flew toward the trunk.

This was my chance. So many trees before me, each spreading its thick branches in upside-down *V*s that could hide me, *if I could just keep quiet.*

Better to choose a tree close by or one farther away? Angela would check the ones close by. On the other hand, she might see me bolting for one farther away.

Angela was pacing toward the sound of that thud. I tiptoed in the opposite direction.

Sheltered under a tree, I pressed against the trunk and watched Angela through the branches. She bent her scrawny legs to peer around the wrong tree for me.

Then she stood, twisted her mouth in an ugly grimace and jeered, "Hiding, Dinah? *As if.* I'll find you. Remember that little-Dinah story you told me? About how you were too red-haired, too loud and clumsy, ever to win at hide-and-seek? How *It* always caught you? Well, I'm *It*," she finished vengefully, "and I'm coming for you."

Stomping over to another tree, she lifted the canopy of pine needles to see if I was underneath.

And, scrunching down, I thought, Yeah, when I was little, I was a lousy hider. What I told you was true, Angela. But here's the part I didn't tell you. The sequel. Little Dinah got older and wised up. She realized that the one with the disadvantage just has to try harder. Has to practice being even quieter and stiller than anyone else.

By grade one, I was the kid *It* never found...

The quieter I grew, the noisier Angela became. In her impatience she crunched on sticks and ripped ferns out of her way. She was only about three trees away, another arrow pulled back and ready to be unleashed.

She couldn't peer around every tree in the forest. I willed her: *Don't see me.* And I imagined bunching up all the energy and noise that was me into a tiny red ball. I pictured pushing it down, down into a deep dark well until it shrank even more. Until it was barely a flicker...

And I thought, I'm not afraid of darkness anymore, Mrs. Cuthbert. Darkness is just the place where your fears live. Visit the darkness, and you conquer it. You make it your own.

The flicker now dwelling in my darkness was a stubborn quarter note that blazed with a red-hot-mama will to live. No cold Bridey revenge for me, but life-giving Galloway fury. Angela wasn't going to *It* me—*because I was going to out-It her.*

Now she was at the next tree. Stretching the arrow way back, she bent to squint through the pine needles. "Dinah," she cooed. "Dinah..." A smile trembled on her pale face. She was enjoying this.

She began sidling over to my tree. In mere seconds, she'd bend, peer in, see me, *zing* the arrow—

As my singing instructor always tells me, there's a time for stillness, and there's a time to let loose the full shock-and-awe of your lung power. I leaped—and from my throat the angry red quarter note, my personal fire of being, soared out and exploded.

"AAAAGGGHHHHH…" It was the strangest note I'd ever sung, more of a wild primal animal cry, and the longest. I crashed Angela to the ground. "BAD NEWS," I yelled, planting my foot on her chest. "THE OLD, UNIMPROVED DINAH IS BACK."

I grabbed the bow from her and threw it aside. Then I proceeded to break or bend out of shape every one of her arrows.

Dazed, Angela scrambled up. Her face was twisted into a snarl. Too late I saw that she gripped the bow. She lifted the aluminum handle way up and started to bring it down on my head—

Whi-i-s-s-s-h-h-h-h… Thwack.

It happened so quickly I thought at first she *had* struck me.

But it was Angela who staggered and collapsed, felled by a well-chewed old baseball.

London reached me before Talbot of the surefire baseball aim did. I gave London her second hug of the day. Just a pure lovely big hug this time. I'd used the first hug as cover for looping the pop-can-ring necklace around London's furry neck without Angela noticing. The pop-can ring, my own personal summons for help from Talbot. As he'd pointed out by Trout Lake, it was the thought behind the metal that counted, not the brand of metal.

"DINAH!" Talbot charged up.

I was so overwhelmed with a mix of emotions— gratitude, relief and, oh, probably a few hormones—that for once in my life I couldn't think of anything to say.

So I tackled him with a mega-bear hug.

I figure that might be what *ebullient* means.

Chapter Seventeen

Not So Queenly After All

Talbot and I hoisted Angela's arms over our shoulders and half dragged, half walked her to the lake. London trotted happily beside us. With the baseball clenched in her teeth, she was letting loose a series of especially horrible, mangled howls. London was very proud of that baseball.

And of the guy who'd secretly returned to Vancouver to spirit her to Salt Spring, away from the clutches of the parks board officer. London kept casting bright glances at Talbot.

At each howl, Angela moaned, but we ignored her. There was too much to talk about. "*You* gave me that note at the Saturday market," I accused Talbot. "You, Scarf Man."

"I wanted you to know someone was watching out for you," Talbot said simply. "What I *didn't* want was to advertise my presence. I promised Shandi, a friend at camp, that I'd stay hidden on this property until she got the owners' okay for me to camp here."

"Can we pause and rewind? Who *is* this Shandi?" But already I felt my jealousy evaporating. What an idiot I'd been. Jealousy: the number-one life waster. Just look at Beak-Nose and Angela.

"Oh, sorry. Shandi lives on Salt Spring. She's been really helpful.

"Anyhow, if somebody *did* report a trespasser, I didn't want you to be an accessory," Talbot continued, confusing me as he always did when he became honorable. "Better you didn't know who your secret pal was. You had enough trouble, what with being stalked by Beak-Nose. Or"—he shot a foul look at Angela—"niece of Beak-Nose, as it turns out. At the market, where everybody catches up on the week's events, I heard about the falling rock.

"Shandi didn't think the owners would object to my staying here. Besides being really nice, they're animal lovers and would understand about protecting London from the big sleep.

"Shandi drew maps of the property, showing where the storage shed was and"—Talbot grinned—"more importantly, where the key was hidden. Inside the shed is enough camping equipment to go on a safari, and a bike so I could go buy food.

"Earlier today, from the grocery store, I noticed you arriving in Ganges. In case you needed protection, I biked after you to Madame Sosostris's, London running alongside. So much for my timing." Talbot grimaced. "When you really needed it, you were less than half a mile from where I was snoozing at my campsite."

"Never mind," I told him. I removed the pop-can ring from London's neck and dangled it. "You showed your true mettle, buddy."

Then I grinned. "So it was *London* who filched the rest of the pie—just like she helps herself to the contents of people's kitchens back home."

"I couldn't stop her in time," Talbot said, with a frown at the pie thief.

His face grew rueful, which meant he was about to be honorable again. "I'm going to pay the owners for the use of their equipment, plus rent for staying here."

Angela was getting awfully heavy. I tried shifting her deadweight arm to a more comfortable position on my shoulder. "Never mind for now about being conscientious," I told Talbot. "Tell me about your parents. Do they know you're AWOL from science camp?"

"I wrote them too," Talbot said solemnly. "But they're also camping—in the Okanagan. So they won't get my e-mail for a while. And when they do..." He shrugged. "I dunno. I can't let London be put down. But then there's my mom's allergies. I can't ask her to spend the next several years in a nonstop sneeze-a-thon. Hey, maybe I could board London at your place?" he asked hopefully.

"Um..." I thought of our cat Wilfred, who would be frightened, not to mention very offended, by the arrival of another pet, and a canine one at that. Then I brightened. "Maybe I could hide London on the premises, like that family did with England's Charles the Second."

This was yet another historical anecdote courtesy of Talbot. The story of Charles the Second, who escaped to France and then got his throne back in 1660, had played a minor part in the last mystery my buddies and I had solved, aboard a cross-country train.

"So how did you figure out I was your secret buddy?" Talbot demanded.

I considered. "Things just came together. Like Pantelli being so casual about dropping his backpack in the water. I mean, normally he carries his junior dendrologist's gear in there: his magnifying glass, camera, plastic gloves, Baggies for taking samples, notebook. He *loves* that stuff. So I thought, What if he'd *meant* to drop the backpack? What would be in there? Something watertight, for sure. The only answer I could come up with was vacuum-packed food. Maybe he was trying to help someone. Maybe *you*.

"And then there was the Howler." I took a deep breath. This talking and dragging Angela was draining my strength. "Everybody else was scared of the howls. They'd never heard them before. So whatever unfamiliar beast was howling had to be a newcomer to Salt Spring. One day I listened to the Howler and realized the beast was happy, not menacing. And because I was already thinking *you* might be here, I thought of London.

"Lastly, Scarf Man. The way he flapped those dazzling scarves at me, I knew he didn't want me to get a look at his face. But there was nothing frightening about him— about *you*," I amended. "So I figured it wasn't the hen woman or Madame Sosostris who gave me the note. It was you."

Talbot nodded. "I guessed Mrs. Cuthbert would bring you to the market. Everyone goes there, Shandi said. So I bought some cheapo scarves and slathered myself with tan lotion, which I topped off with phony teeth and huge shades.

"The hen woman felt sorry for me. She thought I must be pretty hard up to sneak into the market as an underage seller! I asked for a favor, that she send you to Madame Sosostris. I thought if you were having your fortune told—y'know, with eyes shut, communing with spirits and all that—I could sneak into Madame's stall and sticky a note to your arm. I forgot about the strong odds of"—he grinned—"a Dinah-mite disturbance. But I got the note to you anyway."

I finished, "For all that, though, I'm not sure I *figured* out it was you. I think I just knew."

We grinned at each other, and the silence between us said way more than I had.

Angela's head jerked up. "Soppy moments," she snarled. "I HATE SOPPY MOMENTS."

A soppy moment of a very different kind awaited us at the dock. Amid hoarse gasps, Cornwall was wringing water from his T-shirt. He was so weak, he kept stumbling sideways. Finally he flopped on the deck and lay struggling in vain to get up, like a beached whale.

Letting Angela's arm fall, I rushed over to help him up. Angela took this as a cue to begin screeching.

"Cornwall! Look what they did to me—bashed the other side of my head in! I'm a victim of Dinah, her trespasser friend and"—she pointed a trembling, but oh-so-beautifully manicured, finger at London—"the Howler!"

Assuming Angela wanted to play, London dropped the baseball and started running around it. She uttered several friendly *let's-go-frolic* barks at Angela.

Angela shrieked hysterically, "I'm A VICTIM! A VICTIM!"

"Can it, Devilla," Talbot said shortly. He joined me in holding on to Cornwall. "Take slower breaths, buddy. Relax."

Cornwall spluttered, "Knew she was trouble…called the police…trouble…" His bloodshot eyes fixed on me.

"Yes," Angela told me triumphantly. "Trouble's just what you're going to be in, you snooping songbird. Everyone knows trouble's what you *live* for."

Cornwall gasped raggedly. He was trying to talk but couldn't. Instead he clutched my hand.

I said gently, "You were like Roger Bannister, weren't you, Cornwall? The guy everyone laughed at, because it was too absurd that a pale, flabby, ordinary schoolboy would ever be a champion. You believed the best of me, and, like Roger, you found the best of yourself. The Olympic best. *You swam the lake.*"

"Yeah," Cornwall puffed. He was doing what Talbot advised, breathing slower. "Roger Bannister. Yeah." And the faintest grin poked upward at his wan, plump cheeks.

Cornwall hadn't been abandoning me when he strode away from Mrs. Cuthbert's dock. He'd been going to call the police before his swim, as he explained on the boat trip back.

Talbot rowed; I kept an arm around the still shakily breathing Cornwall. Nobody said anything. The police sirens, first distant, then wailing closer, made up for the lack of chitchat.

Angela sat in the bow, shooting glittery-eyed glares at us all.

As Talbot moored the boat, footsteps pounded the boardwalk. Constable Leary, this time with slicked-back, as opposed to bed-head, hair and looking grim rather than kindly, leaped down the dock steps and stomped to the edge. He was wearing black-toned sunglasses, which made him look even more frightening.

"Missy, you're in serious trouble and I'm here to arrest you," he barked.

The problem was, with both Angela and me reflected in his shades, we didn't know which Missy he meant. I, being loudmouthed and troublemaking, assumed it was me, since adults reamed me out so frequently. Angela, on the other hand, perked up and began tattling out lies in a sweet confident tone.

"Dinah tricked me into going across the lake, officer. She lured me up the hill, and then her pal here—who's a *trespasser*," Angela added in a sad, shocked voice, "bashed me on the head. All because Dinah envies my talent. She's *obsessed* with it."

Angela accepted Constable Leary's helping hand up the ladder. Talbot and I just sat, stunned, in the rowboat. Somehow, if you're the one with truth on your side, you're never glib. And Angela kept rolling out the whoppers like a conveyor belt.

"I wouldn't be surprised if Dinah's friend bashed me on the head the first time round. I mean, we all thought it was an accident, but—"

"*But it wasn't*," shouted Pantelli, pounding down the boardwalk to the dock. He waved a huge color photograph at us. "Dinah captured that first head-basher on the camera. After she loaned me her camera—she thought mine was swimming with the fishes—I scrolled through the photos. She snapped you standing under the Garry oak, Angela."

Constable Leary, I noticed suddenly, hadn't let go the helpful hand he'd given Angela. It was now more of a helpful grip—that Angela couldn't pull away from.

Pantelli flapped the photo in Angela's face. "Naturally, since it was a Garry oak, I had a photo place in Ganges enlarge it several times over. I planned to study it through my magnifying glass on the ferry back to Mayne Island.

As soon as the photo came back, I could tell that you were holding on to a yellow rope…and up in the leaves I saw the rope wound around something gray: the rock that you then yanked down.

"Forget the ferry—I went right to the police. Constable Leary was already on his way out the door, 'cause he'd just got *your* call, Cornwall."

"You meant that rock to hit Dinah, didn't you, Missy," Constable Leary told, rather than asked, Angela. "Well, we'll chat about that at the station."

"NO!" Angela screamed. Her features stretched back and became ugly, like a gnarled old woman's. "THAT ROCK WAS MEANT TO HIT ME! IT WAS! *TELL THEM, DINAH!*" She kept screaming as Constable Leary bore her off.

The irony was that, at long last, Angela was telling the truth.

Chapter Eighteen

Dinah's Personal Best

The audience crammed Centennial Park. People sat on the rows of metal chairs that the town of Ganges had supplied, or they stretched out on blankets or stood juggling babies and formula bottles.

"We *are* about promotions," Mrs. Beechum, beside me on the stage, giggled in my ear. She waved a plump hand at the crowd and TV cameras. "We advertised on radio, TV and newspapers: *Come and hear (free!) British Columbia's official singer for the international 2010 Olympics commercials. Performing at Centennial Park, Salt Spring Island, Saturday afternoon.*"

The chairwoman of the 2010 Olympics promotional committee tapped the microphone in front of us. It wasn't on yet. Technicians were still figuring out electrical connections amid a snake-like jumble of black cords on the grass below. "Yo, Dinah! You gonna"—Mrs. Beechum wiggled her ample hips—"get everyone up and jiving?"

"Um," I said. I waved at Talbot and London, sitting with Mrs. Cuthbert on a blanket. Boy and dog were now guests at Cuthbert's Fitness Retreat. Horrified that she'd been harboring the Night Stalker right under her roof, the fitness expert insisted on plying Talbot and London—whom she regarded as superhero-type rescuers—with every kindness she could think of. Library books on British history. Beef jerky and rawhide bones. (I'll leave it to you to deduce who got what.)

Mrs. Cuthbert had even phoned the St. Johns' Okanagan campsite to give Talbot's mom a blistering earful. "It's your moral responsibility to adopt London. This pooch single-*paw*edly saved Dinah," Mrs. Cuthbert lectured, as Talbot and I, listening, grinned wider and wider. We were pretty sure Talbot's soft-hearted mom couldn't withstand an appeal like that, sneeze-a-thons or no.

I grinned now, which Mrs. Beechum interpreted as a *yes* to her question. "With your belt-'em-out voice, you'll have the whole island shakin' its bootie!" she squealed. "Hooo-eee!"

More hip gyrations. Well, the *stage* was certainly shakin', at any rate.

"Um," I said again. I waved at Madge, Mother, Jack and my agent, Mr. Wellman, who'd all ferried over for this moment of triumph in my career. This peak, this apex, as Mr. Wellman kept enthusing. As the official 2010 Olympics-commercials singer—the opera commercials had been canned after Angela's arrest—my showbiz success was guaranteed. Never mind about any more movie songs with barking dogs or TV appearances with flying pies.

Nearby, with his large, scowling mother, sat Cornwall. He didn't look very happy. His mom had bawled him out for remaining my understudy rather than replacing me. Despite this, Cornwall managed a wave back at me. A good sport, I thought. A true Olympian, just like the original ones Talbot had described from way back in 776 BC, when King Ifitos got all the other kings to sign a treaty agreeing that, as long as the games were on, nobody could fight. That people would strive to be the best they could be.

Over the past few days, Cornwall and Talbot had done lots of talking about the Olympics, and about Roger Bannister and other athletes who'd met daunting challenges.

I thought of my own Olympic challenge, to shed ten pounds. This morning, an official 2010 Olympics doctor had arrived at Mrs. Cuthbert's, armed with an official 2010 Olympics scale.

Suspenseful silence as I stepped on it.

"Same weight as before," the doctor declared.

Briefly, Cornwall's face lit up. Briefly.

"*But you've grown two inches this past month!*" the doctor exclaimed. "You pass the test, Miss Galloway. Congratulations!"

Then there was the other challenge I'd set myself this month: to detect where Beak-Nose was hiding. Well, I'd found out where the *junior* Beak-Nose lurked, at any rate. And the police had nabbed the senior Beak-Nose yesterday—at a florist's, of all places, in Montreal. Seems Violet Bridey had a thing for orange begonias. Noticing a beak-nosed "nun," in full habit, trying to shoplift a pot of them, the florist called security.

A horrible ripping sound seared my eardrums; the huge speakers on the Centennial Park stage were now activated.

Mrs. Beechum grabbed the microphone and started gushing into it.

"TESTING, TESTING." More ripping sounds. Everyone cringed. The techies plugged more cords into outlets. Ahhh, relief. The ripping faded. I removed my hands from my ears.

Mrs. Beechum shouted into the mike: "Welcome, citizens of Salt Spring! Welcome, visitors! Yoo-hoo, welcome all you people in TV-land!" She waved at the cameras. "Today I, Alma Beechum, am proud to present to you two performances of 'British Columbia on Fire'!"

Uneasy stirrings in the crowd. The BC-wide drought was still on. "Oh, not *that* type of fire," Mrs. Beechum scolded. "The Olympic-torch-type fire! 'British Columbia on Fire' is our official song of the Olympics commercials! And today, débuting the song, will be the two finalists for the starring role in commercials to be shown around the world! In Venice, along the canals…in St. Petersburg, beside St. Isaac's Cathedral…"

Not this again. It'd been bad enough listening to her United Nations roll call with Madge that day over the phone.

"…in Stockholm, by the—"

"WHAT ARE YOU, AN ATLAS?" somebody shouted. A female voice, and a familiar one, though not one I often heard raised in anger. No, it couldn't be. Elegant Madge, heckling? I stared down at my sister, who looked back at me, all innocence. Jack, however, was laughing.

Wow. You never knew what to expect with people you thought you understood. Which brought me back to Cornwall. Who'd have predicted that arrogant, nasty, attention-craving Cornwall Blutz would turn out as heroic as the athletes he admired, if not more so? That he would risk a possibly fatal asthma attack by swimming St. Mary Lake?

Mrs. Beechum glowed. "You'll hear first from our front-runner, Dinah Galloway, the red-hot redhead of show business. According to 2010 Olympics promotional committee rules, Dinah just needs to sing 'British Columbia on Fire' publicly—and she's it! The star! So get ready to dance in the aisles everyone. This is gonna be one rousing performance!"

A fireman stepped forward. "Actually, there *aren't* any aisles, Mrs. Beechum. And that brings me to a concern about overcrowding. I—"

"Unbelievable," Mrs. Beechum muttered to me. She drowned out the fireman with "LET'S HEAR IT FOR OUR OFFICIAL SINGING REPRESENTATIVE, DINAH GALLOWAY!"

An explosion of clapping. I figured people were glad to be rid of Mrs. Beechum, so I didn't take the applause and cheers as personal flattery. How could I? Most of these people hadn't heard of me. My showbiz résumé consisted of the musical version of the *Moonstone* (my "apex" so far, as Mr. Wellman would say), the singing-salami radio commercials, my pie-laden TV appearance and a movie title track vying with a barking dog.

But starring in the 2010 Olympics commercials would change all that. No wonder Mr. Wellman was beaming at me from the front row; ditto Mother, Madge and Jack. This'd be my ticket to fame. Through the commercials, my voice would vault around the world—I'd get all kinds of offers and become an international success.

I stepped up to the mike. At the side of the stage, techies were cranking up the CD with the opening notes of "British Columbia on Fire." I'd practiced the song with

Talbot strumming guitar; I could belt it out, no problem. That was me, that's what I did, that's how I expressed the oomph-packed, emotional, one-girl marching band that was Dinah Galloway.

I sucked back a deep breath, preparing for the first knock-'em-dead note of "British Columbia on Fire." I mean, so what that I didn't really care about the Olympics—at least, not the way Cornwall did.

Through his Roger Bannister book, Cornwall had studied—more like inhaled—the dream of performing one's personal best according to Olympics tradition. Just the way I'd relived Judy Garland's triumph, after years of setbacks, at Carnegie Hall. Performing at Carnegie Hall, *Crumbly* Hall as I'd called it when I was little: now that was *my* dream.

And it occurred to me that meeting an Olympic challenge, achieving your personal best, wasn't a triumph of the body. Nope, no matter how much you exercised and even bullied your muscles into shape. It was a triumph of the heart. It was a belief in doing what was finest, for yourself and others.

"Dinah," Mrs. Beechum hissed from the side of the stage. "You missed your opening notes. Start the music again," she snapped down at the techies.

The audience members were glancing at each other and shrugging. My family and friends leaned forward, their faces anxious: What was wrong? Dinah Galloway never missed a cue. Mr. Wellman looked especially worried.

The introductory notes started again. I knew that the new, improved Dinah would carry on, just as she was supposed to.

But then I remembered the red-hot quarter note that had blazed in the very well of my being when Angela was after me in the forest. It was a stubborn note, a survivor, an *individual*.

And it knew a true Olympic challenge when it butted up against one.

Man, the trouble I was about to get into! I gave Cornwall a wobbly grin.

And walked off the stage.

Velma, a.k.a. Madame Sosostris, was dragging a purple-painted table across her lawn. A teapot and cup jiggled on top, along with a sign: CURBSIDE TEA LEAF READINGS BY MADAME SOSOSTRIS, $5. She gave a shriek when she saw me. "You again! Now looky, I'll call the police on you, I will. *I've had enough.*"

"A lot of people feel that way about now," I nodded. "Right up to and including the government of British Columbia, so I'm told."

Or, more accurately, so I'd been screeched at. Mrs. Beechum's tirade—"Ungrateful, irresponsible…I'll black-list you in the theaters of Vancouver…in the bistros of Victoria," etcetera, etcetera—had followed me along Ganges's main street.

By now, though, she'd be fussing over the new official singer for the 2010 Olympics commercials, Cornwall Blutz.

I sighed, wondering if singing with dogs and dodging pies would be the apex of my career after all.

"Hmph," said Velma, slightly softening at my glum expression. "Is it that bad?"

"Bad hasn't even started," I said. "I'm barely in the *warm-ups* to bad."

I handed her a chocolate-drizzled scone in a Salt Spring Roasting Company bag. I'd bought it on my way to her home. "This is for you, by way of an apology. I'm sorry about tearing off your wig and then impersonating your client. I didn't mean to."

"Hmph!"

I straightened her CURBSIDE TEA LEAF READINGS sign. "'Madame Sosostris,'" I repeated. "Cool name. My mother would like the T.S. Eliot touch—if she ever speaks to me again."

"You *are* in a bad way," Velma said. Long purple skirt flapping about her skinny legs, she nipped over to her carport, grabbed two patio chairs and dragged them over to the table. "Siddown, you poor kid. Tell you what, I'll give you a free reading. *Sometimes* my predictions are right, y'know." And she cackled.

I slumped into the guest chair, more to be polite than anything. I didn't believe in fortune-telling. On the other hand, the Madame Sosostris quotation had proven strangely accurate:

> *And here is the one-eyed merchant, and this card,*
> *Which is blank, is something he carries on his back*
> *Which I am forbidden to see.*

I'd known there was a stalker on the island, but her calling card had been blank; I hadn't guessed her ID till it was almost too late.

And Mother, ever bookish, had pointed out that Angela fit the "one-eyed merchant" description as well. In mythology, "one eye" represents jealousy. As for being a "merchant," well, Angela *was* a merchant of sorts. She'd been trying to sell her singing, just like Cornwall and I did.

Though whether *I* ever could again, after today's captured-on-TV walkout…

"Oh, stop sighing," Velma tsked. "The stars will only communicate with us if we *concentrate.*"

She shook some wet tea leaves from the pot into the cup. "Now, let's see what patterns the leaves form, what predictions they hold…"

But as she set the pot down, Madame Sosostris accidentally rammed her elbow into the bag holding the chocolate-drizzled croissant. The delicate pastry fell apart, scattering its pieces out of the bag, over the table.

"Dang   it!"   the   fortune-teller   exclaimed. "All crumbly…"

Melanie Jackson has written five previous Dinah Galloway mysteries, which have been heralded by *Resource Links* as "a great hit for mystery buffs everywhere. Excellent." Melanie lives in Vancouver, British Columbia, and is working on another Dinah Galloway mystery.

Praise for the Dinah Galloway Mystery series

The Spy in the Alley

Young mystery fans will look forward to Dinah's further
cases. Highly Recommended.
—*CM Magazine*

A fun lighthearted story that also deals thoughtfully with
serious issues.
—*School Library Journal*

...leaves us wanting to see much more of the Galloway family.
—*Children's Book News*

A great hit for mystery buffs everywhere. Excellent.
—*Resource Links*

The Summer of the Spotted Owl

My nine-year-old has just inhaled all four. His message to
Jackson: MORE!
—*Georgia Straight*

The book offers readers lively dialogue, a well-paced
narrative, an action-packed plot, an appealing heroine...
Highly recommended.
—*Canadian Book Review*

Dinah's smart-alecky self-deprecating personality will carry
readers through to the satisfying conclusion.
—*School Library Journal*

...difficult to resist such an irrepressible character.
—*VOYA*

Young readers will like her quirkiness and the twists and
turns of this surprisingly unpredictable plot.
—*KLIATT*

Shadows on the Train

Jackson has crafted a mystery that evokes and blends the best
of Gardner, Hitchcock, and Christie.
—*KLIATT*

Other titles in the Dinah Galloway Mystery series

The Man in the Moonstone
978-1-55143-264-9
$8.95 pb
ages 9-12 208 pages

Other titles in the Dinah Galloway Mystery series

The Mask on the Cruise Ship
978-1-55143-305-9
$8.95 pb
ages 9-12   192 pages

Other titles in the Dinah Galloway Mystery series

Shadows on the Train
978-1-55143-660-9
$8.95 pb
ages 9-12 208 pages

Other titles in the Dinah Galloway Mystery series

The Spy in the Alley
978-1-55143-207-6
$8.95 pb
ages 8-12 192 pages

Other titles in the Dinah Galloway Mystery series

The Summer of the Spotted Owl
978-1-55143-412-4
$8.95 pb
ages 9-12 192 pages